EVERYTHING
BUT A BRIDE

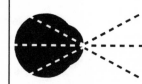

This Large Print Book carries the
Seal of Approval of N.A.V.H.

EVERYTHING
BUT A BRIDE

HOLLY JACOBS

THORNDIKE PRESS
A part of Gale, Cengage Learning

WYNDHAM CITY
LIBRARY SERVICE
P.O. BOX 197
WERRIBEE VIC. 3030

GALE
CENGAGE Learning

Detroit • New York • San Francisco • New Haven, Conn • Waterville, Maine • London

LIBRARY OF CONGRESS CATALOGING-IN-PUBLICATION DATA

Jacobs, Holly, 1963–
  Everything but a bride / by Holly Jacobs.
    p. cm. — (Everything but series : no. 2) (Thorndike Press large print gentle reads)
  ISBN-13: 978-1-4104-1551-6 (alk. paper)
  ISBN-10: 1-4104-1551-1 (alk. paper)
    1. Hungarian Americans—Fiction. 2. Weddings—Fiction. 3. Domestic fiction. 4. Large type books. I. Title.
  PS3610.A35643E9 2009
  813'.6—dc22
          2009002577

Published in 2009 by arrangement with Thomas Bouregy & Co., Inc.

Printed in the United States of America
1 2 3 4 5 6 7 13 12 11 10 09

My *Everything But . . .* series is
about family.
This book is for my family:
my parents and
for my brothers Rob, Rick, and Mike
and their families.

PROLOGUE:

THE SALO FAMILY
WEDDING CURSE

"Tell us a story, Nana Vancy," five-year-old Chris Wilde begged as his great-grandmother tucked him and his brother under the covers.

"Tell us about when you were a girl," his dark-haired twin, Ricky, added. Vancy Bashalde Salo knew the story, and she knew that they loved it because it had everything to do with how their uncle and aunt got married.

"I was a beautiful girl. I'm not bragging when I say this, because it is the truth. Many men in my town —"

Chris interrupted. "Erdely, Hungary."

Nana Vancy nodded. "Yes, Erdely, Hungary. And many of the men my age wanted to marry me, because I so was beautiful. My hair was as black as yours and your Aunt Vancy's and my eyes as blue. Yes, many men wanted me, but only one would do."

Ricky supplied, "Papa Bela."

She nodded. "I only had eyes for Bela Salo. I was lucky back then, and Bela fell in love with me too. He wanted to marry me. My father was the mayor, and he encouraged me to plan the biggest wedding the town had ever seen. I was sure everything would be perfect."

"But Papa Bela didn't show up," Chris said.

"Right. My Bela wasn't there. I thought he had abandoned me. I was heartbroken and angry —"

Chris nodded. "So you said the words."

I hope Bela never gets a big, beautiful wedding like this." She could still remember the pain of that day, when she thought her Bela didn't love her. Even now, all these years later, even knowing the truth, it hurt.

"And you said, you hoped no one in his family had a big, beautiful wedding, 'cause it would make you remember you didn't get yours," Chris prompted when she got lost in the past and stopped the story.

She nodded, back in the present, looking at her oldest granddaughter's two stepsons. Well, not stepsons, exactly. They were her granddaughter, Vancy's, husband, Matt's, nephews. Vancy and Matt were raising them, and the boys were sons in their eyes, which made them great-grandsons in her own eyes. With their dark hair, anyone would take them for her actual grandsons. And they were grandsons in her heart. That's all that mattered.

"Right," she continued. "I said the words because I was hurt and couldn't stand the thought of watching my Bela — and his someday children — have the wedding I didn't get. But in my pain, I forgot that words have power."

"And when you remembered, you went into the woods and said . . ." Ricky waited.

"I said I wanted to undo that curse. But if I couldn't take back the words cursing Bela and his family to unhappy weddings, then I asked the powers-that-be to let me add that it wasn't my intention to curse Bela or his family to lives without marriage or love. Just no big weddings that meant more than the marriage itself."

She admitted, not for the first time, "I'm afraid that's what happened to me. I thought more about the wedding than what came after. So I asked that the curse be broken when the day came that someone in Bela's family cared more about love and their marriage than about the actual wedding."

"Then Papa Bela came back," Ricky said. "He'd been in an accident."

"I was so happy to see him, so happy to

know he really did love me, that I never thought about waiting for another big wedding. No, that very day we found a minister and got married, just the two of us and our best friends there to witness it. I didn't think anything else about those words I'd said until my own children all missed out on their big weddings for one reason or another."

"And you wanted to break the Salo Family Wedding Curse when Uncle Matt married Aunt Vancy," Chris said.

"But they didn't wait," his brother chimed in. " 'Cause they were in *lo-o-ve.*" He said the word *love* with such a singsongy emphasis that both boys started to giggle in that little-boy way.

Vancy couldn't help chuckling herself. "Right. But now your Uncle Noah is getting married, and I'll break the curse at that wedding, because he doesn't care at all about the ceremony."

She couldn't believe her luck. The curse would be broken in only a few short weeks because neither Noah nor his fiancée, Julianna, cared about the wedding. They'd left all the details of the ceremony to her. It would be a beautiful wedding, but that didn't matter to Noah and Julianna, so that meant that as soon as they'd said their "I do's," the curse would be broken.

She'd brought the curse down upon her family, and one way or another she was going to see it lifted.

Two weeks from now the Salo Wedding Curse would be gone forever.

"And after the wedding there won't be any more curse," Chris said. "And we'll have cake."

"Chocolate cake, right, Nana?" Ricky asked.

The chocolate cake had been the boys' request. "Yes, a big, beautiful chocolate cake. And there will be singing and dancing . . ."

Nana Vancy forgot that her story was supposed to be inducing the boys to sleep as she got lost in rhapsodizing about the upcoming wedding.

"And we'll all live happily ever after," Ricky said.

"Yeah, that's the best story ending."

"You're right, it is," Nana Vancy said. She leaned down and kissed the twin foreheads. "Now, that was a very long story, so I expect no monkey business. Both of you straight to sleep, or I'll be in trouble with your aunt and uncle."

"We'll go right to sleep, Nana. Night," Chris said.

The two boys closed their eyes, and Vancy Bashalde Salo made her way out of the room, switched off the light, and shut the door.

Two more weeks and the curse would be lifted. She'd planned everything.

Nothing could go wrong.

Could it?

CHAPTER ONE

Noah Salo hadn't wanted a stag. When Darren Duffy, his college roommate and best man, insisted, he'd finally agreed, but only if it was a coed party. He'd thought that if his fiancée, Julianna, was there, it would be more fun.

He'd been wrong.

Darren had booked a private room in one of Erie's trendy bars, located downtown on State Street. And when Darren used the word *trendy,* he meant loud and pretty much wall-to-wall people. Their private room was filled to the brim and overflowing into the main bar. It was wall-to-wall people Noah barely knew.

No, this was not his idea of fun.

Julianna was lost somewhere in the mob, having the time of her life. He was glad she was happy.

She often complained about his less-than-exciting tastes in entertainment. A good book, an occasional movie, a trip to the beach, or skiing in the winter — all of those constituted time well spent in Noah's book, especially when Julianna was with him to share the pleasure.

But this?

Well, he'd get through the next few busy weeks, and then life would return to normal. Quiet and orderly and pretty near perfect with Julianna by his side, as his wife.

They'd decided to hold the wedding at the end of January because Noah worked for his family's company, Salo Construction, as the business manager, and the construction business slowed to practically a standstill in the middle of an Erie, Pennsylvania, winter. The city sat on the southern side of Lake Erie and was prone to lake-effect storms. Cold Canadian air blew over the lake and dumped truckloads of snow onto the city, either slowing any building process or making it grind to a complete halt.

It was a perfect time to get married. But the festivities surrounding his wedding were not his idea of a perfect time. Still, all he had to do was get through the stag, the wedding, and the reception, and next week he'd be tucked away in a romantic mountain lodge with his wife.

Wife.

He loved how that word sounded.

"Hey, Noah, come on. You can't hide in a corner all night at your own stag." Callie Smith, his soon-to-be sister-in-law, stood grinning at his side. She and Julianna weren't biological sisters. Julianna's mother had married Callie's father when the girls were twelve and ten respectively. Callie's father had adopted Julianna a few years later. Maybe that explained how night-and-day different they were.

Tall, blond Julianna liked to be surrounded by activity. She loved parties like this one. Loved to be on the go, whether it was traveling or shopping. She loved being in the thick of things. She was always dressed to the nines, and Noah was pretty sure, other than during an occasional dip in a swimming pool, he'd never seen Julianna without makeup.

Callie, on the other hand, was tiny, about five foot three, and rarely bothered with feminine touches. She claimed that no amount of makeup would cover her freckles, and she insisted that her reddish brown hair had a life of its own and that the best way to counter its wandering tendencies was to braid it into captivity.

But tonight she'd foregone the braid, and

her hair cascaded wildly about her shoulders. She must have put on some makeup as well, because there seemed to be fewer freckles visible, though Noah knew they were hiding somewhere. The result was rather disconcerting. She didn't look quite like the little sidekick he was accustomed to.

"Come on, Noah. Julianna and your buddy Darren have dragged most of the party out onto the dance floor. They're tripping the light fantastic, as my grandmother used to say. You've got to come out too."

Okay, he was trying to be a good sport, but dancing? He shook his head. "I can't dance."

"Oh, come on," Callie insisted. "Everyone can dance. Just move your hips to the beat, and swing your arms a bit. That'll work in a pinch."

"Callie, I have no rhythm. None. In fact, if there's an opposite of rhythm, that's what I have. I can swing my hips, but it never even comes close to matching up with the beat of the song. Remember Elaine on *Seinfeld*?"

"That bad?" she asked in mock horror. She couldn't sustain the expression for long. Her ever-present smile overpowered her within seconds. "We've been friends all these years, and you've kept this terrible affliction hidden?"

Noah couldn't help but grin as well. "I'm worse than Elaine," he assured her. "But since you and I rarely hang out anywhere that could lead to dancing, it's not such a shock that you didn't know."

"Listen, if I could let Julianna drag me to the beauty salon — aka the dungeon of torture — and make me sit for two hours while some lady toyed with my hair, putting so much stuff — oh, pardon me, *product* — onto it that it now officially weighs five pounds more, you can certainly make an effort to dance."

"Seriously, it would be worse than torture to everyone who had to look at me."

"Did I mention that Julianna made me wear makeup too? She spent half an hour putting some kind of cover-up foundation on, trying to camouflage my freckles. She wasn't successful, which made her a bit testy. Have you ever tried to keep your eyes open while a testy woman wands mascara into place? If I can survive that, you can dance."

"But —" Noah started to protest again, but the look in Callie's eye said that this once he'd get no sympathy from her.

"Okay, here's the deal. There's bound to

be a slow song coming up soon. Come out with me then, and follow my lead. No one will be the wiser. We'll turn a few simple circles, then head off the floor."

"But —"

"Come on. You don't want to hide in the corner for your entire party, do you?"

Noah had known Callie since she was young. She'd frequently tagged along with him and Julianna during her weekends and holidays with her father. She was a great sidekick and later a good friend. And he knew that she'd long since figured out how to wheedle him into doing whatever she wanted.

"Please?" she urged.

Admitting defeat, Noah nodded. "Your boyfriend won't mind your slow dancing with me?"

"In case you never noticed, no one, not even Jerry, tells me what to do. Plus," she added with a grin, "he doesn't dance."

"Hey, so why does he get off the hook and I get dragged onto the floor against my will?"

"Because it's your party, and as the host you have to dance. Jerry is a guest. There-fore, there is no obligation for him."

"I don't think that's fair."

"Ah, but if Jerry and I get married, you

can force *him* to dance. Retribution of sorts. But tonight it's *your* party, and you're dancing."

"You're still as bossy as ever, I see."

She grinned as she shrugged. "It's a curse."

"Oh, not you too. That's all my grandmother's been able to talk about since Vancy's wedding — the Salo Wedding Curse and how it's up to me to end it."

"My 'curse' was an expression, but Nana Vancy truly believes in hers. The fact that you and Julianna are allowing her to plan your wedding in order to break it — well, that's very nice. I mean, I don't believe in curses, but it will put her mind at ease."

"Well, I don't care much about the ceremony per se. And you know I'm not keen on parties —"

"Or dancing," she interjected with a grin.

"Or dancing. I'd actually have preferred to elope, but Nana was so insistent, and despite the fact that you'd think she'd want to be in the thick of wedding planning, Julianna assured Nana Vancy that she didn't care." He shrugged.

"Well, it was nice of you both," Callie said as the current song came to a stop and a new one, a slow one, began. "I think that's our cue."

Feeling like a man marching to the gallows, Noah followed her onto the dance floor.

As he took her into his arms, it struck him anew that Callie was a tiny thing. Every time he noticed, it seemed incongruous that someone with such gusto for life, with such a big heart and so much drive, was packaged in such a tiny body.

He tucked her quite comfortably under his chin as they danced. *Dance* was actually a generous description. He followed Callie's lead in what was basically a giant circle, nothing that truly tested his lack of ability.

He spotted Julianna dancing with Darren. She gave him a wave and smiled, though the expression didn't quite reach her eyes.

Something was wrong. He could see it, but he couldn't, for the life of him, put his finger on what it might be. Julianna had seemed quiet and not quite herself for a while now. Every time he asked, she assured him that nothing was wrong.

"Is something up with your sister?" he asked Callie.

She pulled back and looked up at him. "I don't think so, though she's been a bit subdued lately."

"She doesn't look quite right."

"It's probably pre-wedding jitters."

20

"You think?"

"I'd be nervous and out of sorts if it were me."

He tried to picture Callie in a poufy white dress, walking down the aisle and into some man's arms, and frowned. He couldn't quite manage it.

Callie had a boyfriend, had had others, but none of them lasted, which was fine with Noah, since none of them had really been men he'd want to see Callie end up with. She deserved someone special. "I can't imagine your getting married."

"Hey, that's not nice."

"No, I didn't mean I couldn't imagine any guy wanting to marry you. I can easily imagine that. But I can't imagine one of them who would be good enough for you."

"That's a little better." She sounded mollified, and when she smiled at him, he knew he was out of trouble. "You're getting better at digging yourself out of a hole, Salo."

"Which is good, since I so frequently find myself in one. Things never come out quite the way I intend."

He stopped dancing as Julianna approached them. "Hey there, my future wife."

He leaned forward to kiss her on the lips, but Julianna pulled back and twisted, and his kiss landed chastely on her cheek.

"Noah, can we talk?"

Callie laughed and singsonged, "Uh-oh, Noah's gonna get it."

Noah saw Callie look at Julianna, and all teasing died.

"Something wrong, Jules?" Callie asked with genuine concern in her voice.

Julianna didn't answer. She shook her head and said, "Later," then turned to Noah and added, "alone."

"Thanks for the dance, Callie." He left Callie standing on the dance floor and followed Julianna.

Noah wasn't the most astute man in the world, at least when it came to females, and he knew it. As he'd told Callie, things didn't always come out right. But astuteness and an eloquent tongue wouldn't be enough to save him from whatever it was Julianna was about to rail at him about. He recognized the signs. Her back was tense, her expression grim. She wasn't even trying to hide that she was upset.

"Honey?" he said as they both wove their way across the dance floor.

"In private" was her only response as she picked up her pace, leaving him nothing to do but follow.

She led him out of the club through a back door. They walked into an alley. It was freezing.

A dim light near the street barely reached them at the rear of the club. But even the darkness couldn't hide the huge Dumpster or the trash that had long since overflowed it and now littered the ground, and even the cold weather couldn't keep it from smelling.

"Honey, maybe we should find somewhere else to talk. Neither of us is dressed for this weather, so let's —"

She interrupted him. "I can't do it."

He could make out her features but not well enough to confirm the tears he thought he heard in her voice. "Do what?" A sinking feeling settled into the pit of his stomach.

"This. Go through with this. I just can't. I thought I could, but I was wrong."

"The party? That's fine. You know I'm no fan of this type of thing. I only said yes because I thought you'd enjoy it. We'll sneak out now and go home."

"Not the party. The whole thing." Her voice softened to almost a whisper. "The wedding."

"Oh, man, Julianna, you scared me. You know I don't care about the wedding. I only want to be married to you. It was sweet of you to let Nana plan it, but I don't think either of us thought she'd go this overboard.

We'll call it off and fly to Vegas."

"That's just it, Noah. I don't want to fly to Vegas and marry you either. I thought I could do it. I do love you, though I'm sure you're going to have a hard time believing that when I'm done here."

She paused a moment, took a deep breath, and said in a rush, "I know I'm twenty-six, and we've been dating forever, so marrying you seemed like the next logical step, but . . ."

"But?" The word fell on him like a brick.

"But I don't think I love you the way I should. And if you were honest, I don't think you love me the right way either."

He realized Julianna was calling off the wedding. He'd always expected they'd marry. They'd dated through high school, had known each other all their lives. He'd always planned for a future that included Julianna. And now she was telling him she didn't love him the right way?

"There's a right way to love someone?" He waited for the pain to strike, but he couldn't seem to find it underneath the anger.

Julianna reached out to touch his cheek, but he jerked back.

She sighed, and more than ever he was sure she was crying. Most of the time the thought of Julianna's crying made him want to pull her into his arms, but right now he didn't want to touch her.

"I'm making a mess of this," she said softly. "I know I am. I knew I would. The thing is, I don't think we're right for each other. I believe you love me, and though I'm sure you're going to doubt it for a while, I do love you. But not the way a wife should love a husband. It's more like the way a sister loves a brother. Yes, that's it exactly. It's the way Dori loves you. Warm and fuzzy, not hot and steamy. And I want hot and steamy."

"Julianna, you've got the pre-wedding jitters."

She shook her head, and not a perfect blond hair moved from its place. "No, I wish that was all it was. There's so little time until the wedding, but we're going to have to cancel. I wouldn't want to leave you at the altar the way Vancy got left."

"Julianna, let's give this a day or two —"

She shook her head. "A day, a month, a year — it wouldn't matter. I can't marry you, Noah." She tugged off her engagement ring and tried to hand it to him, but he wouldn't take it. She finally grabbed his hand and forced the ring into it.

"I'm sorry, Noah. I can make the calls and

send the notes if you like. I'll have Callie call Nana and see what I need to do. And I'll pay whatever money we lose."

He found his voice. "Money? You think money matters when the woman I love is leaving me?"

"I'm not leaving you, Noah. I'm just not marrying you. I know I should have come to this conclusion earlier, but I *wanted* to love you the right way. I've been waking up with panic attacks for months. And tonight, as I danced with Darren, I realized I just couldn't do it."

"This is about Darren?" He couldn't believe his college roommate would steal his fiancée.

"No, it's about me. This is all about me," she said in an earnest voice. "Noah, I'd like to stay friends, because even if you don't believe it now, I do love you. I know you can't see that right now, but I hope that, after some time, you will."

"Yeah, I know, you love me like a brother. The way Dori or Vancy loves me." He shook his head. "Sorry if that's not exactly comforting."

"Noah . . ."

"I'll let you go back inside to tell everyone. I'm leaving."

He trudged through the slush, past the

Dumpster, and toward his car. He should have offered to go in with Julianna and tell their friends together. But he couldn't. The life he'd dreamed he'd have had just been shattered. He needed time to sort it all out and figure out where he was going to go from here.

Callie listened to her sister make the announcement that the wedding was off and thank everyone for coming.

"Hey, Callie, do you suppose this means we get back the money we paid for the stag tickets?" Jerry joked.

Sometimes Callie wondered why she dated him.

He must have sensed he'd gone too far, because he quickly backpedaled. "Hey, just trying to ease the tension with a joke."

"Jokes are funny. That wasn't."

"You're upset about your sister. Don't take it out on me."

She didn't have time for a fight with Jerry; she had to catch her sister. "Hey, try to find your own way home with one of the guys," she called to him as she ran after Julianna.

Because so many people were stopping her sister, offering their sympathies, she didn't have much trouble reaching her.

"Pardon us," she said, extricating them

both from the crowd and leading Julianna outside onto State Street. "My car's down there," she said, not worrying that she'd brought Jerry and he'd be left to his own devices.

They got in, and Callie started the engine, turning the heat up to high before she turned to Julianna. "So?"

"I couldn't do it. I know marrying Noah made sense, that everyone expected it, but, Callie, I don't love him like a wife should love a husband."

"You broke it off with *him?"*

Julianna nodded.

"I'm sorry, Jules. I know that had to be hard, but . . ." She paused, feeling more than annoyed with her flighty sister but knowing that Julianna needed her comfort now, not a lecture. "But better to end it now than go through with a wedding you're not certain about."

"I think Nana Vancy's right — there *is* a curse on the Salo family. I simply didn't imagine it was me."

This time Callie's comfort was genuine. "Hey, enough of that kind of talk. You're not a curse. And though Noah's sure to be hurting" — she hated to think about how much pain he must be in — "it's better to end it now than find out you were right after you'd made your vows."

"I *am* a curse. I've suspected for a long time that I didn't love him the way a wife should love a husband. What's wrong with me? How could I not love him enough? We've dated since I was old enough to date. We were friends before that. All my life, actually. He's a great guy. Seriously, he's probably one of the nicest guys I've ever met. He deserves so much better than being left at the altar."

"You didn't do that. It's two weeks until the wedding. You left him at the stag. There's a difference."

Julianna chuckled, which had been Callie's intent. Oh, it was a weak chuckle, but it was there nonetheless. "Now, what can I do, Jules?"

"Can you check on Noah? I told him I hoped we could stay friends, but I think that might take a while. And there's all the wedding plans to cancel. Nana Vancy has most of the information, and I can't imagine she'll want to talk to me, so if you could get it from her, I'll start making calls."

"How about this? I check on Noah, and I get together with Nana Vancy and take care of all the cancellations."

"I couldn't ask —"

She'd been so annoyed when Julianna told

her, but, listening to her sister, she realized that Jules was hurting too. "You didn't ask. I offered."

Julianna reached over and hugged Callie. "I was going to wait until I took care of undoing all the wedding plans to get away for a while, but I can leave immediately if you're sure."

Callie nodded.

Julianna sighed. "Thanks, Callie. You're the best."

"I know," Callie teased, and she was rewarded by another weak smile. "Where are you leaving for?"

"Nowhere in particular. I just need to try to figure out . . . what now?"

"If you need me . . ." Callie let the offer hang there.

Julianna nodded. "I know, I know. You're here. You've always been here. I was thrilled when our parents found each other, but I don't think I realized at first that they were giving me the best gift ever — a sister. Even though you only lived with us on weekends and vacations, you were my sister."

"Hey, none of that, or we'll both start crying." Callie knew it was dark enough that Julianna couldn't see it was too late; tears were already pooling in her eyes. She brushed them away. "And, if I recall correctly, you didn't always enjoy having a weekend sister."

"You grew on me." Julianna paused, then added a well-used line. "Like a fungus."

They both smiled at the old joke, which didn't seem as funny as it normally did.

"Could you give me a ride home, then go check on Noah?" Julianna asked.

"Yes." Callie turned and put the car into gear. She was glad that Julianna had suggested it, because even without her sister's prompting, heading over to Noah's had been her next stop.

CHAPTER TWO

Noah continued to ignore the phone.

He had ignoring it down to a science. That's what two weeks of solid practice could do for a guy, especially when the darn thing had been ringing incessantly for every single one of those last fourteen days.

He hadn't wanted to talk to anyone two weeks ago, and he didn't want to talk to anyone now. He wished his friends and family could understand that he wanted some time to figure out what went wrong.

No, not just wanted, needed.

But even more than that, Noah wished his grandmother hadn't sent John Warsaw, a reporter from the local paper, an invitation to the wedding. His grandmother had wanted to prove to the reporter that the Salo Wedding Curse had indeed been broken. After Noah's sister was jilted at the altar, Warsaw had written a story about the Salo family's wedding curse, a story that was then picked up by other papers.

The Salo Family Wedding Curse had become national news and had driven his sister, Vancy, into hiding.

And the fact that the curse had struck again seemed to not just reignite the flames but fan them into a full-fledged bonfire. Noah felt as if he were standing in the center of it as he dodged reporters, left and right.

SALO FAMILY WEDDING CURSE STRIKES AGAIN, Warsaw had written. Again the national media had run with the story, making the last two weeks an utter nightmare.

Someone knocked on the door, but Noah ignored that as well. He went to work laying a fire in the stone hearth. Normally he had fires for the ambience, but today it was for a more practical reason — it was cold out.

Freezing cold.

The sky was dark and ominous, which worked for him, since it perfectly matched his mood.

The doorbell rang.

He was absolutely not going anywhere near the door. Odds were it was a reporter, his mom, his grandmother, or one of his sisters. He loved three out of the four possibilities but didn't want to talk to anyone.

The nice thing about guys, they knew

33

when to leave another guy alone. His father, grandfather, and brother-in-law, along with all his friends, had respected his need to be on his own for a while. Too bad the women in his life hadn't.

"Hey," a voice called from the living room doorway.

For a moment he thought it might be Julianna, coming to say she was sorry, that she'd simply had a case of cold feet. But he turned and saw Callie standing there instead.

When he was mentally listing the women in his life who wouldn't allow him to wallow in his depression, Callie should have been at the top of his list. She'd been more of a pest than his grandmother — and being a bigger pain than Nana Vancy was quite the accomplishment.

"How'd you get in?" He knew how rude that sounded but didn't seem to be able to help himself. He turned back to the fire and lit it before standing and facing his uninvited guest.

"I know where the key is kept, remember?" Her face was red from the cold, and she'd obviously already taken off her outerwear and boots, because she stood in stocking feet, which made her seem even tinier than usual.

"And it didn't occur to you that by not answering the door, I was implying I wasn't up for company?"

"No." She walked into the room, flopped onto the couch, and propped her feet on his coffee table. A coffee table Julianna had helped him pick out.

Noah realized how many things in his house — in Erie in general — reminded him of Julianna.

"I'm not company," Callie stated.

"No, you're a pain in the a—"

"Tsk-tsk," she interrupted. "That's no way to talk to a friend."

"So say what you must, then get out."

She took her feet off the table, planted them firmly on the floor, and leaned closer to him. Noah suddenly remembered that Callie had been there the day he'd bought the coffee table. She'd helped Julianna pick it out. He wasn't sure why he remembered that; it didn't have any relevance to the lecture he was sure Callie was getting ready to deliver.

"I didn't come to say anything." She leaned forward enough to put a hand on his knee. "I came to check up on you."

"I'm fine," he assured her, though he knew it was a lie. He was adrift, trying to figure out what direction his life was going to take now. For as long as he could remember, he'd thought he'd marry Julianna, have some kids, and they'd build a life together. Now? He didn't have a clue.

"I'm glad you're fine" was all Callie said.

They sat in silence, neither feeling the need to speak as they watched the fire. Noah decided that lighting it had been a mistake; it looked far too cheery to suit his mood.

He glanced at Callie, and she smiled at him. He didn't smile back. She was even more cheery than the fire, and that was making him feel more morose.

The phone rang.

"Are you going to get that?" she asked.

He shook his head. "It's probably just more reporters."

"Yeah, I saw that the press picked up the wedding curse story again. I'm sorry."

"I don't think I gave my sister, Vancy, enough sympathy when she had to deal with it. Although, I don't think it's been as bad for me. A cursed groom isn't as big a story as a cursed bride."

Since Callie came in, Noah had used more words than he'd used since the stag. He felt as if he'd used them all up and fell silent.

Callie tried to think of something to say, something that might lift Noah's spirits, but

her own spirits were in the depths, so she
wasn't overly successful. The best she could
come up with was, "Your grandmother and
I took care of everything. You guys are out a
bit of money, but Nana's a tough negotia-
tor. Other than deposits, she got a lot of it
back."

Noah shrugged. "The money doesn't matter. I told your sister that."

At the mention of Julianna, he looked at
her, and she could read the question in his
eyes.

She'd hoped to avoid talking about
Julianna but knew he wanted — no, needed
— to hear. "She's fine. She left town for a
while, but she calls. She's worried about
you. So are your family and friends. And
me."

"I'm fine."

"Yeah, yeah, yeah, I know. You keep saying
that to anyone who manages to breach your
fortress of solitude long enough to talk to
you. But I don't care how much you say it,
I don't believe it, because I'm not fine."

"Huh?"

He looked confused, not that Callie was
surprised. Noah had rarely been able to follow her conversations, and this one took a
harder-than-usual tangent, since she hadn't
given him all her news. "I broke up with

Jerry last night. Or at least that's the story I'm putting around. Truth is, I caught him with someone else, so I broke up with him, but it wasn't as if I planned on breaking up with him."

"Sorry." For the first time since she'd come in, Noah looked something other than depressed or angry. He looked concerned. "Are you okay?"

"I'm fine," she said, echoing his catch-phrase.

He laughed. Well, at least he attempted to laugh. It came out more of a *garphump* than a true laugh, but, given the two weeks he'd spent moping, she'd take it.

They sat in companionable silence for a long while, just watching the fire as it consumed the wood, turning the entire pile into a bed of glowing embers.

"I couldn't get the money back for the honeymoon," Noah finally said.

"Sorry," she said.

"I decided that, rather than waste it, I'd go. I figure a week away from here, away from the reporters, away from all the memories, away from everyone, might be what I need to clear my head."

Callie didn't mention that he'd been hiding out away from everyone already, and it hadn't helped. "Good for you. I wish I could get away. I wasn't about to marry Jerry, but still, it stings."

Actually, it more than stung. Callie finally had to admit, after walking in on Jerry and his bimbette, that she couldn't keep a man. The last three had all cheated on her. There was something wrong with her that made men stray.

Jerry had told her that he was sorry. He hadn't meant to hurt her, and he'd still like to be friends.

Friends.

That was the problem. Men tended to see Callie as their buddy, their pal. A friend. She knew they'd truly liked her and had tried to convince themselves they could see her as more, but in the end, they couldn't. None of them.

It had to be her stupid freckles. Or maybe it was the fact that girly behavior had never sat easily on her. She hated messing with her hair and makeup. She didn't get all fluttery over jewelry or new clothes. Give her a functional pair of jeans, a weather-appropriate top, and a pair of sneakers, and she was good to go.

Yeah, men found it hard to picture her as anything more than a buddy.

She let out a depressed sigh.

"I've got an idea," Noah said, suddenly

turning toward her and smiling.

"Last time you said that to me, your idea involved stealing a FOR SALE sign and putting it on Ms. Lewis' front lawn."

"Hey, I was only thirteen, and it sounded like a good idea at the time." He laughed.

The sound warmed Callie more than the fire did. "And I was only ten and ended up in even more trouble than you did once my dad picked me up."

"How was I supposed to know that her son was a police officer? I mean, she was Ms. Lewis, not Mrs. Lewis."

"All I know is that my dad about did me in after that little stunt. I've been leery of your great ideas ever since." Despite being depressed about her latest louse of an ex, Callie couldn't help but feel a bit lighter, knowing she'd made Noah laugh.

"Here's the thing. I have the honeymoon suite at the Maple Grove Inn up by Peek 'n' Peak. I figure a week there will keep the press and well-meaning family away. The thing is . . . well, I've got to confess, the idea of staying in it by myself is less than appealing. What if I see if they'll let me exchange it for one of the cottages, and you come along? We can do some skiing, maybe some hiking . . . just like the old days."

She'd known Noah since her father married Julianna's mother. The three of them had become inseparable, except when it came to the outdoors. Then they did separate. Julianna would send the two of them out on hikes or fishing, and she'd go to the mall and shop or get her hair done. Noah, who had only sisters, treated Callie like the little brother he'd never had.

"Come on," he said. "You can keep me from moping, and I'll do the same for you. We can both get away from everyone's wanting to know how we're doing and just relax."

"Are you sure?" The idea seemed promising, but Callie had this little niggle of a feeling that there was some basic flaw in his plan. "You're sure it's a good idea even to go? You don't think it will make you more depressed about Julianna?"

"Listen, I think getting away from here, from the constant barrage of my family's concern, is just the ticket. And I can't think of anyone I'd rather go with."

It sounded so good, so reasonable, as he said the words, but that niggle wouldn't stop. "And you'll get a cottage. I'll have my own room."

"Yes. If I can't, then we'll just forget it."

She looked for another reasonable reason to say no. "Well, you know, getting off work might be iffy."

"I know your boss." He laughed.

Since Callie worked for Salo Construction, it wasn't an issue. She'd started working for them over summer breaks from high school, then from college. She had a degree in business but loved working with her hands. There was something so satisfying about looking at a house and knowing she'd had a hand in building it.

She didn't feel as if her degree had gone to waste, though. She ran a nonprofit foundation in her spare time and felt that both jobs combined her skills nicely.

"My boss is a real ogre," she needled Noah, who ran the business end of Salo's. His sister, Vancy, handled the legal aspects, and the youngest sister, Dori, was a hands-on employee like Callie. "I mean, he's really strict and kind of scary."

He laughed. "I know he is, but I still think I can pull a few strings."

All teasing aside, she pointed out, "I've never used preferential treatment before."

"You've never caught a boyfriend with another woman before."

She didn't bother to correct him on that statement. One boyfriend cheating on you was sad; three was pathetic. She wasn't about to advertise the fact.

"That deserves a few days off," he continued. "And think of it this way: I'm representing the male population, trying to show you that not every guy is a rat bastard like Jerry."

The idea of getting away from it all for a few days and just kicking back and recovering from her bruised heart appealed to her. Well, maybe not a bruised heart. Maybe it was just bruised pride. She'd suspected for a long time that Jerry wasn't going to be the man of her dreams. But she hadn't expected him to move on to his next woman until they'd officially broken up.

"Well, then, on behalf of the female population, I accept your attempt to make up for all lousy males out there."

"Great. Pick you up tomorrow at eight? It's not that far. We'll be there in time for brunch, then a day's skiing."

"Sure. You're on."

Noah woke up the next morning and realized something was different. He looked out the window at the still-dark landscape and saw that the weather was the same. The sky was that winter-brilliant black, with a thousand tiny stars breaking up the expanse. A sliver of moon cast the barest of lights on his snow-covered backyard.

Everything was the same.

He walked through his quiet house, knowing that he'd expected to have Julianna living here by now, filling up the empty spaces with her things. He came from a large, loud family. He hadn't realized until he'd moved out to Greene Township, out of the city of Erie proper, how still true quiet could be.

Nothing had changed. The house remained just a house, not a home he was sharing with someone he cared about.

He realized he'd thought the word *cared.* Not *loved.*

Of course he loved Julianna. They'd been an item since they were kids. He'd always expected to marry her. He'd bought this land, built this house, and planned to live here with her.

Even thinking about Julianna and how quiet his house was didn't dim the new feeling that sort of welled up in the center of his being, a place that had been so cold and hollow for the last two weeks.

That's when he realized what he was feeling was plain, old-fashioned anticipation. He couldn't wait to load up the car, strap his skis to the rack, and go pick up Callie.

He loved the outdoors. Maple Grove not only promised him some great skiing at the neighboring resort, Peek 'n' Peak, but it had an ambience that would have pleased Julianna. Quaint, cozy, and filled with all that froufrou stuff that had always delighted Julianna. It had been the perfect compromise for them.

He didn't have to worry too much about the froufrou elements with Callie. She'd always been more at home in jeans and work boots than dresses and heels.

His sense of excitement grew as he packed the car and headed off to pick up Callie. There was no waiting for her to get ready, to finish packing, to put on her makeup. Instead, she opened the front door of her Grandview Boulevard condo as he pulled into the drive.

"Morning!" she called out, as she wheeled a small suitcase with one hand and tucked her ski bag under the other arm.

"That's it?" He shouldn't be surprised. He'd gone on outings with her in the past, but, still, this was a whole week. "You're sure?"

She looked at her things. "Yes, unless there's something I don't know about."

"No. I should have known better. It's just that I've gotten used to women who pack for a weekend trip as if it were a Continental tour."

"Not Dori."

"No, my sister is sensible. But the rest of my family and yours —" He didn't want to talk about the rest of Callie's family. Well, at least one specific member of it. He didn't even want to think of her.

"Let's just get your stuff stowed, and we'll be on our way. I'll treat you to brunch before we get there."

"Great. I had some cereal, but that's hardly enough to hold me for a day of skiing."

He laughed. It felt good. It felt normal. "Your eating abilities have always amazed me. I don't know where you put all that food."

"I work hard, and I figure that as long as I work it all off and don't end up sitting on it, it's all good."

Callie started to chatter about this and that, little bits of minutiae.

And about half an hour into the trip Noah realized he'd laughed more in the last thirty minutes than he had in . . . Well, he couldn't remember how long.

This trip was a great idea.

CHAPTER THREE

The Maple Grove Inn was a huge Victorian-looking white clapboard building. A wide porch wrapped around it as far as Callie could see as they drove in. The lobby was ornate and decorated in a Victorian style. It was fancier than Callie generally felt comfortable with.

But as Callie followed Noah, who followed the bellman with the baggage cart down a blacktop path to their cottage for the week, she realized that the outbuildings were nothing like the main inn. They passed numerous log cabins as they walked the recently shoveled path. They dead-ended at the last cabin, and the bellman walked onto the porch and opened the door with a flourish.

"Welcome to Rose Cottage. We at Maple Grove Inn want you to consider this your home for the week and to count on us to do everything in our power to see to it you have a wonderful stay. The master bedroom with its king-size bed is in here." He threw open the door to a rustically elegant room. The logs that formed the cottage made up two of the walls. A huge stone fireplace was opposite the quilt-covered bed. The furniture itself was big and substantial, a perfect match for the rest of the décor.

"And a second bedroom, also with a king-size bed, is here," the bellman continued, opening the door next to the master bedroom's door. This room didn't boast a fireplace but otherwise had the same feel to it.

"Each room has its own private bath. The master bath is equipped with a spa tub and a working gas fireplace. You also have the fireplace in the living area."

He indicated a stack of papers and brochures on the coffee table. "And since you ordered the all-inclusive package, you'll find your itinerary, as well as brochures about the particular activities, there for your inspection. We hope you enjoy your stay with us here at Maple Grove Inn, and if there's anything I haven't covered, or if you have any questions, please don't hesitate to call your personal concierge, George." He said the name with an odd little accent and handed them George's card.

Noah slipped the bellman a tip, which the

man happily pocketed as he left.

"When you said *cottage,* I expected . . . well, a cottage. We've got the Taj Mahal here."

"You know your sister." At the mention of Julianna, Noah's expression dimmed. "I really worked to find a place we'd both enjoy. It was great that this was so close to Erie. I've skied at the Peak for years but never really checked out this resort."

He thumbed through the itinerary. "All our meals are included, and tomorrow I booked Julianna a day at their spa. You might as well use it."

"Spa?" There were many things Callie had always wanted to try. Bungee jumping. Hang gliding. But going to a spa didn't even come close to making her list. Being poked, prodded, and basically beautified for a day sounded like her idea of torture. "Really, you can just cancel it."

"Like I said, it's paid for, so you might as well go enjoy it. Aren't you the one who's always encouraged me to try new things? When I swore I wouldn't work for the family, you coaxed me to give it a try, and I found, rather than hating it, I liked it and was good at it."

"So, I should try spa-ing because you've got a head for business and I was astute enough to notice it?"

"You should try it because you deserve a day of being pampered."

"And what will you be doing while I'm being 'pampered'? And by *pampered,* you know I mean *tortured.*"

"I'd planned on doing some skiing, then, uh . . ."

He'd been smiling at their teasing, but that smile suddenly died, and he looked decidedly uncomfortable. And that made Callie decidedly uncomfortable as well. "Go on, spit it out."

"Well, I'd booked a couple's massage at three."

"No, don't cancel. If I've got to be spa-ed all day, then you can keep the massage at three. Just call and let them know there will be no coupling with it. We'll meet when you're done."

He looked relieved. "Great. Our dinner reservations each night are for six. I didn't schedule anything for today, so we have the whole afternoon in front of us. Why don't we unpack and hit the slopes over at the Peak? The inn has a shuttle that runs back and forth every half hour."

"Great."

Callie shut the door to her room, needing a moment of privacy. She could hear Noah just on the other side of the wall by the bed. The exterior walls might be made of logs, but the interior one separating the two rooms wasn't so thick. As a matter of fact, she could hear his every movement well enough to be pretty sure that the interior walls were paper-thin.

It shouldn't bother her. After all, it was, in fact, a wall. But hearing him move about and unpack left her feeling rather exposed on her side, so she walked through the room on tiptoe and opened drawers as quietly as she could.

When Noah had suggested this trip, she thought it sounded like a perfect way to get over her heartbreak and help a good friend get over his. But on the car ride up, she'd begun to wonder if, in fact, it was such a good idea.

They'd been friends for years. They'd played together as kids, hung out as adults, but nothing in their history had been quite as intimate as a week in a cabin together.

She heard him shut what she assumed was the closet door. A moment later she heard him open his bedroom door, walk the couple of steps that separated their rooms, and knock.

"I'm ready whenever you are," he said.

"I'll be right out."

Without the distraction of listening to him, she finished unpacking in short order, changed into her ski outfit, and grabbed her skiing equipment. "Done."

He whistled. "You are the fastest woman I've ever met."

"Uh, would you like to rephrase that? I don't think it came out quite the way you intended." She gave him her mock stern-teacher look, one that her English teacher, Miss Mac, used to give the class. She even went so far as to cross her arms and tap her foot.

He laughed, not the least bit intimidated. "What I meant is, I don't think I've ever fully appreciated how non-girly you are. I mean, you're like one of the guys."

All sense of humor fled at the words. Even though she knew he didn't mean telling her she was "one of the guys" as an insult — that to him, and to most men, those words were offered as a compliment — they hit too close to home, too close to the reason all her relationships seemed doomed to failure. It was hard for a guy to get serious about "one of the guys."

"Gee, thanks," she muttered.

"Callie, did I say something?"

"Yes, of course you said something. You gave me that sublime compliment. And

52

since I'm 'like one of the guys' and ready so fast, let's get this show on the road and get some skiing done."

She grabbed her ski bag and walked toward the cabin door.

"Listen, I know I'm not always the most astute guy around — Julianna told me so all the time — but I'm sorry if I did something or said something that upset you. You know that wasn't my intent."

She sighed and turned back toward him. Standing there in his black ski pants and red and black jacket, a black hat pulled down over his equally black hair, and looking so little-boy forlorn, she felt embarrassed to have reacted so strongly to something she knew he'd meant kindly. There were many things about Noah she'd always loved, and his kindness was a big part of that.

Girls had always chased him. He was almost six feet tall and had dark good looks, but he'd never noticed. He never realized how good-looking he was.

Callie realized she was being overly sensitive, and she wasn't sure why. "Listen, it's not you, it's me. I'm out of sorts."

He walked over and put an arm around her shoulders. "We're both out of sorts, and we have cause, so we'll just take turns cheering each other up. Right now, it's my turn to cheer you up."

"And how are you going to do that?"

"I'm going to take you skiing, and after a few runs down the mountain, I'm going to buy you a hot chocolate at the lodge, and I'm going to slip the waiter a big tip to make sure that our mugs have at least half whipped cream."

As quickly as it came, Callie's funk lifted, and she laughed. "You'd do that for me?"

"I know you, Callie Smith. You say you love hot chocolate, but I've always known it was the whipped cream that made the drink for you."

"Well, come on then. The sooner we get to the hills, the sooner I get my hot choc— whipped cream."

Whatever oddness had assailed her as she unpacked disappeared as she and Noah hit the slopes. The resort had a great base down, and the weather was cold enough for nice powder but not so cold that she lost feeling in her extremities.

Callie breathed in the snow-scented air as she whipped down the hill. Noah would laugh at her and tell her that snow didn't smell, but she'd argue that it did. It was a crisp sort of scent that spoke of cold and pine trees, of fresh air and freedom.

Freedom.

It had been a long time since she'd felt that way. She'd had serial boyfriends for the last five years, one after another, looking for something in them that she never found. She wanted someone who liked the outdoors. Someone who didn't mind that she was allergic to dressing up. Someone who liked to read and could carry on intelligent conversation that ranged from politics to television.

"Hey, Callie, you're putzing!" Noah yelled as he careered past her, laughing, daring her to try to catch up.

She laughed and leaned into her skis.

Someone like Noah, she thought, finishing her internal conversation.

Yes, if she could ever find someone who understood her as well as he understood her, she'd scoop him up.

"Watch your back, Salo!" she called as she caught up to him, laughing.

Yes, the next man she dated would have to be more like Noah and less like her exes.

Later that night, Callie snuggled into the couch and pulled a quilt up over her. "I think I'm getting old. I don't know when it happened, but somewhere along the line I slipped up and aged, because no one who's not old should hurt this much after a day of skiing. Granted, I haven't skied in a few years, but that doesn't excuse the kind of pain I'm feeling right now."

Noah glanced over his shoulder at her as he was lighting the fire. Though he'd never admit it, the day had taken its toll on him as well.

"I don't think you can possibly qualify as old if you're still in your twenties. But maybe it's a good thing you've got your spa day tomorrow. I've got to confess, I'm looking forward to the massage. I called about putting us in two separate rooms."

The idea of having someone work out the kinks in her back and her thighs almost made Callie weep with appreciation.

"Had they dealt with couples who want to uncouple for their couples' massage before?"

"I dare you to say that sentence again." He started back toward the other end of the couch.

"I don't think I could."

As Noah started to sit, she cautioned him, "Gently. Sit on this couch very, very gently. If you can manage that without causing me excruciating pain, I'll give you half the quilt."

He sat down so softly, the couch didn't

even jiggle, and she dutifully kicked some of the blanket his way.

"Want to watch something on TV? We can rent movies."

"Sure. You pick."

"Chick flick?"

She laughed. "You know better than that. Wasn't there a new espionage film out a while back? Maybe it's out in pay-per-view."

Noah skimmed through their choices, found the show in question, and selected it. "Ready?"

"I'd nod my head, but it would hurt too much, so I'll just say yes and go back to feeling old."

"Just remember, massages tomorrow. We'll both be ready for the slopes again after that."

"Massage. Massage. Massage. That's my mantra for the night."

The movie was good, but the day in the snow had taken its toll on Callie. One minute she was watching a car chase through the streets of Paris, and the next thing she knew, Noah was gently shaking her by her shoulders. "Callie. Come on, time for bed."

Noah wanted to take her to bed? No, that couldn't be right.

Callie's sleep-fuzzed mind tried to make

sense of what he was saying. Slowly she managed to pry her eyelids open. And found herself face-to-face with Noah. He was smiling. Despite being fuzzy, she knew it was good to see him happy again. And she smiled back at him as she stretched and tried to clear her mind.

"What did you say?"

"I said it's midnight and time for bed." He paused a moment and asked, "What did you think I said?"

She shrugged and regretted it. "Ow."

"Want me to rub your shoulders? They hurt from using your poles. It's a different set of muscles than you use on a day-to-day basis."

Without waiting for her to respond, he gently massaged her shoulders in a slow, methodical manner.

"You don't know how good that feels," she heard herself murmur. It felt like heaven, his hands slowly, firmly rubbing away the knots in her muscles, his face just inches from hers. He needed to shave, having gone way past five-o'clock shadow to midnight stubble. She wanted to feel it rasp against her hand. She wanted to trace his lips with her fingers, and then, when she was done, she wanted to lean in and . . .

Realizing what direction her mind was

headed in cleared away the last of her nap-induced fuzziness. She shut off the fantasy and stood, pulling herself out of Noah's reach and almost knocking him down in the process.

"Sorry," she said. "Uh, we'd better go to bed now."

He nodded. "It's getting late. You're right. We'd best get to bed. We've got a full day in front of us tomorrow."

He seemed totally oblivious to the weird, aberrant fantasy she'd just indulged in. For that, Callie was thankful beyond belief.

"Come on, I'll walk you to your door." He draped an arm around her shoulders, as he'd done for years.

But this was different. She wanted to shrug out from under his arm, but she didn't want to alert him that anything was wrong, so she let it stay in place and tried to ignore that having him hold her, even so casually, felt nice. Felt right.

Which was not the way it should feel. What on earth was wrong with her?

"Don't you need to make sure the door's locked, or turn off the fire?" she asked, hoping he'd move his arm. She was ready to bolt the moment he did.

"Watch." He flipped a switch as they walked by the fireplace, and it turned off.

"It's gas. Cool, huh?"

"Cool," she agreed, knowing there was no escape unless she was willing to explain why just last week his arm over her shoulders wouldn't have made a blip for her, but now it was different.

He walked her right to her door and opened it for her. She started in, but he grabbed her arm and stopped her. "I just wanted to thank you. I figured today would be a disaster, but I had a great time. I should have known better. I mean, I always have a great time with you. You're a good friend. And I appreciate everything you've done." So saying, he leaned down and kissed her cheek in a platonic, brotherly sort of way.

He stood there waiting, as if expecting Callie to say something in response. She couldn't think of anything to say — except *kiss me again, and mean it* — and the fact that she wanted Noah, her newly dumped friend, to kiss her made all other thoughts evaporate.

She finally managed to say, "Good night," then hurried into her room and shut the door firmly. Only then, in her dark room, did she allow herself to gently touch her cheek, where Noah's lips had just been.

He'd kissed her in the past. Friendly,

platonic pecks between friends. Why was this one affecting her this way? Why did she want something more?

Years ago she'd had a crush on him. A schoolgirl sort of crush that had long ago died when it became obvious that he only had eyes for Julianna and that he'd only ever see her as a friend. And, of course, that's all she wanted.

She'd come here to support him, to help him recover from Julianna.

Julianna.

She felt sick as she thought about her sister.

For a moment, a brief moment, she'd forgotten all about her sister and the pain she knew Julianna was going through. She dug through her bag and found her cell and speed-dialed Julianna.

"Were you asleep?" was her salutation.

"Sleep? What's that?" Julianna laughed, but there was no humor in the sound. It was hard and filled with pain. "How is he?"

"He seems better. We skied all day, and that seemed to help."

"You two always have thrived on that sort of stuff. Personally, I'd rather get my nails done than spend a day out in the cold."

"I just wanted to check on you," Callie said.

What she really wanted to say was, *I almost kissed your ex-fiancé, and I'm sorry.* But she realized the words would only make Juliannna feel worse and wouldn't really appease the guilt that was eating away at her.

"I'm as fine as I'm going to be. He didn't deserve what I did to him."

"You can't make yourself love someone if you don't. It was kinder that you ended it now, rather than having to divorce after the wedding."

"We never did make sense as a couple. I love him. I know he won't believe it, but I do."

"Even if he doesn't believe it, I do."

"Thanks." Julianna sniffed. "If I could have picked someone to fall in love with, it would have been him. But . . ."

"*But.* If there's a but, there's a but. You can't help how you feel." Callie had been spouting that sort of platitude to her sister for the last two weeks. She was beginning to feel like a country-music radio station.

You can't make yourself love someone.
You can't help how you feel.
If there's a but, then run.

But as a title, "I Wanna Kiss Your Ex-fiancé" wasn't one she was going to share with Julianna. Oh, no, she'd call that one the "Bad Sister Blues" and keep it to herself.

Instead of confessing, she simply said, "Just wanted to check on you and say I love you."

"Just take care of him. He's always been so happy when you're around. The two of you have so much more in common than the two of us ever did. I don't know why you and Noah didn't hook up instead of us."

The guilt got even worse. "We didn't hook up because I was always the pest who tagged after the two of you."

"You were never a pest. The day our parents got together was the best day of my life."

"Same for me, Julianna." Callie needed to get off the phone before she said or did something she'd regret. "Listen, I'll call you tomorrow."

"I'm fine, Callie. Just take care of Noah."

Callie clicked her phone shut, feeling more guilty than ever. *I don't know why the two of you didn't hook up,* Julianna had said.

Back when she was younger, she'd have given anything to have Noah see her as more than a pest. But gradually, as she got older, she became accustomed to being his buddy and pal. Men didn't fall for pests. Or buddies. And she'd long since recovered from her crush.

That little moment in the hall was just a

sleep-induced blip in the history of their friendship. And as long as she was the only one aware of that blip — and she was — it was all good and fine.

Nothing had changed.

Nothing was going to change.

She was here this week to cheer him up, and, let's face it, she was here to let him cheer her up. That's what friends did.

She refused to think about the weird aberration in the hall and instead decided to take a shower, hoping that the hot water would soothe her aching muscles. Twenty minutes later, she did indeed feel better.

She walked back into the bedroom proper and eyed the bed with delight. There was something utterly decadent about a huge bed made up with fine linens. It was her one girly weakness. Her bed at home had soft, plush Egyptian sheets and a huge quilt she'd picked up one Sunday afternoon with Noah.

They'd gone out to Mill Village to an Amish mill that supplied some specialty woods he wanted for a project. On the way they'd spotted a small white house with a hand-painted sign proclaiming *For Sale: Quilts, baked goods. No sales Sundays.*

She remembered Noah's laughter when she practically begged him to stop the car and back it down the dirt road to the quaint white clapboard house with its tin roof. Chickens had been pecking in the side yard, and there was a huge barn with a corral and a big draft horse.

The woman who'd answered the door with a baby in one arm and a toddler hanging on to her leg had shown Callie dozens of quilts. After debating with herself, Callie had chosen a pale green and yellow wedding-ring patterned quilt.

She smiled at the memory. Though her bedroom at home was plush and comfortable, this bed went a step further. There were a half dozen pillows and a duvet covered in a flannelish brown slipcover. She pulled it back and almost squealed with delight at the soft sheets. She slid in and covered herself, wiggling around until she had the bedding just so.

She closed her eyes, sure that the decadence of the bed, accompanied by a hard day of skiing, would have her asleep within minutes. Seconds ticked by as she stared at the ceiling and waited impatiently for sleep to claim her.

Callie had already noted that the interior walls of the cottage were thin, but what she hadn't counted on was just how thin they were. She could hear the television in the next room murmuring.

She listened a moment, then decided that was fine. She often fell asleep with the TV on at home. As if by some perverse sense of timing, Noah chose that moment to turn off the television.

Even better, she thought, resnuggling into the bedding and noticing a soft creak as she did so.

Then she heard another creak, this time from Noah's room. She could picture him doing much the same sort of positioning.

She closed her eyes and a moment later heard more creaks coming from the other side of the wall. She listened a moment. Nothing.

She sighed and closed her eyes.

Creak.

Half an hour later, she realized that Noah was having a hard time sleeping. And because he couldn't sleep, neither could she.

She wondered if she should knock on his door and try to find some excuse to talk to him.

No, she decided. There was no way she was knocking on Noah's door tonight.

Or any other night.

CHAPTER FOUR

The next morning, Noah felt as if there was grit under his eyelids, and he blinked rapidly, hoping maybe that would help, but it didn't. So he settled for a long sip of coffee, hoping that would be enough to make up for his rough night.

He had no idea why he hadn't been able to sleep. But he quickly realized that though the inn was beautiful, it also had the thinnest interior walls ever. Because he was a builder, he knew that the walls between the bedrooms should have been insulated, not for heat but for sound. He'd bet there was nothing but air between the two pieces of drywall, and not a lot of air at that.

He'd heard every move Callie made — and she'd made plenty.

That was another thing. The inn had obviously skimped on the beds themselves, because hers creaked horribly.

Over and over, creaking and groaning as

she tossed and turned.

He took another sip of his coffee.

"Morning," Callie said. At least that's what he thought she'd said. It sounded sort of gruntish.

"Not a morning person?" he teased.

She turned and glared at him, wild-eyed and sleep tousled.

"So, what your answer is is, no, you're not a morning person?"

This time her response was simply a growl. She whirled around and went to find the coffee. She cradled the warm mug in her hand, slowly sipping the brew.

"So, are you excited about your spa day?" He wasn't sure why he was teasing her, but when she looked up and stuck out her tongue, he felt practically chipper despite his lack of sleep.

"You know, Callie, most women would be thrilled at the idea of being pampered for a whole day, yet you look as if you're on your way to the gallows."

"I think it would be wise if you were quiet while I brace myself for today with some coffee."

He was quiet as she drank her brew and watched as with each sip she looked more awake. She took a second cup with her into her room to get dressed.

They walked in companionable silence to the main building.

"I could still cancel," she offered as they reached the porch. "You might need me."

"I'll be fine, Callie, though I appreciate your concern. I mean, I'm sure the only reason you'd cancel is because of me." He laughed.

She didn't. "But I'm supposed to be cheering you up," she maintained stubbornly. "I can't do that if I'm being poked and primped all day."

"I'll feel cheerful thinking about your being pampered. Remember, I'm supposed to be cheering you up as well. I think this might be just the ticket."

"A ticket to sheer torture."

"Callie, it's all right to be a girl sometimes."

"I don't mind being a girl — never have. It's just that I'm more at home on a construction site than in a day spa."

"Listen, if you really don't want to —"

She sighed. "I'll give it a try. But I'm telling you, the first person who whispers the word *wax* to me, I'm out of there."

He laughed again. "Deal." Then he sent her through the spa doors and realized he was on his own for the day.

Now what?

Having Callie come along on this trip was a god-send. He'd be at a total loss without her. But he could manage a few hours on his own. Skiing would make the time pass faster.

He headed back to the cabin to pick up his ski stuff. He'd just opened the door when his cell phone rang.

He chuckled as he answered it. Callie had already wussed out on the spa day? That had to be a record of some kind. "Callie, come on, be a man. It's just a facial."

"Noah."

That would teach him to look at his caller ID before answering the phone. "Nana Vancy."

"Where are you?" Her voice was sharp. Nana might be getting older, but she was still head of the family, no matter what his grandfather or parents might want to think. "I was at your house yesterday and again today."

"I decided to get away for a bit."

"Do you know where Callie is? Her mother called this morning, and it seems she just picked up and left town. Dori said she asked for a week off work, and you know that's not like Callie. Dori, of course, said yes but didn't ask why. Her mom says she's not answering her phone and that she was supposed to close on a new house for HOMEs, but she pushed that up to next week — also out of character. I said I'd find her."

Callie had started HOMEs with his grandfather's help. *HOMEs* stood for *Housing for Metro Erie.* The foundation bought dilapidated inner-city properties, renovated them, then, in partnership with local banks, sold them to first-time, low-income home buyers.

His grandfather, Bela, consulted, but it was Callie who ran the show, in addition to working full-time at Salo's. Salo Construction volunteered on projects frequently. He knew, as well as Callie's mom and his grandmother, that Callie didn't take time off from work either on a construction site or especially on HOMEs.

He scrambled to think of a plausible explanation, something his grandmother would buy. When nothing came to him, he opted to not explain but simply say, "She said she was going out of town."

"Yes, we know that. She took off, and no one seems to know where. Your sister Dori might know, but she can be so incredibly closemouthed sometimes."

He was going to buy Dori a lovely gift this week. He wasn't sure why Callie was dodging calls and hiding her whereabouts, but if he had to guess, he'd guess it had something to do with the possibility that no one in their collective families would understand that this was simply a platonic week together.

"Maybe she just needed some time away as well."

"Her boyfriend broke up with her, and her mother's afraid Callie's taken it hard. You know Callie's track record with men isn't very good. She never seems to hold on to one. Her mother wants to comfort her daughter."

"I understand, but I don't know what you want me to do."

"Come home so I can comfort you. Then you can help find Callie. Everyone will be comforted, and we'll all feel better."

"I feel fine, Nana Vancy. I've adjusted to the situation."

"You forget, I had a broken heart once, when I thought your Grandpa Bela didn't love me. I know what that pain's like. It doesn't just disappear in two weeks and leave you 'fine.' Losing a true love alters you in some fundamental way for the rest of your life. You need your family around you, comforting you and helping you find a way to go on."

Noah was struck by how wrong Nana

Vancy was. And she was rarely wrong. But right now, he didn't feel crushed, didn't feel as if his life was altered in any permanent way.

He'd planned to marry Julianna, it hadn't worked out, and he was recovering nicely, enjoying a week on the slopes with a friend.

And maybe the fact that he had recovered so quickly meant that Julianna was right — they never should have planned to marry at all. "Nana, really, I'm fine. I'll be back at the end of the week, and I'll call you then."

"And I'll come comfort you with a big pot of my Hungarian dumplings. They've always been your favorite."

His grandmother had long been a believer in the restorative powers of food — especially Hungarian food. "Thanks, Nana. I'll call when I get home."

"And you'll call if you hear from Callie?"

"Nana, Callie's a big girl. If I hear from her, I'll tell her to call home, that her parents are worried. But I'm not running and tattling on her."

"Fine. And, Noah?"

"Yes?"

"I'm sorry." There was a hitch in his grandmother's voice that made him think she might be crying.

"Nana? Sorry for what?"

"For the curse. First my words almost destroyed Vancy, now you. My curse is no longer ruining weddings, it's ruining relationships. If I don't break it with you grandchildren, I don't want to think about what it will do to your kids."

"Nana," he said gently, knowing she really believed her curse was at fault, "the reason my engagement to Julianna failed had nothing to do with you and everything to do with the fact that we didn't love each other the way we should — not like you and Papa Bela, Mom and Dad, or Vancy and Matt do. And I'm thankful that she was brave enough to call it off and make me realize that."

"But —"

"No buts, Nana. Despite the fact that it hurt, Julianna was being a good friend when she saved us both from making a terrible mistake."

And as he said the words, he realized how true they were. If he'd married Julianna, it would have been the biggest mistake of his life. He wanted what Nana and Papa had, what his mother and father had, and Vancy and Matt had. If he couldn't have that kind of love, then he'd rather stay single.

He'd be the family's bachelor uncle. He'd give all his nieces and nephews fabulous gifts and dote on them. He'd make Salo Construction an even bigger success because he'd be able to devote all his time to the business.

He'd go to the park and play chess with his cronies.

That's right. That's what old bachelors had — cronies, not friends or buddies or pals.

He'd buy man sandals — mandals — and wear them with socks and the wide array of Bermuda shorts he'd have to go invest in.

His grandmother sniffed, interrupting his bachelor plans. "Thank you for saying so, Noah, but I still know where the blame lies."

"The blame is with Julianna and me for thinking a good childhood friendship was anything more than it really was. I'll talk to you at the end of the week, Nana Vancy."

He hung up and, rather than heading for the slopes, sat down on the couch and stared out at the snow-covered landscape.

He'd known there was something wrong with his reaction to their breakup. He'd taken it far too well.

He should have felt rage. Or grief. Instead, he'd been left with some nameless emotion he hadn't tried to analyze. Now he was able to identify what it was he had felt: relief.

He loved Julianna — he knew he did —

but maybe he wasn't in love with her. Maybe she'd been right, and their love wasn't the stuff his parents and grandparents had. Maybe it was the love of two friends.

No maybes about any of it.

Julianna and Callie had been part of his life since his school days. Julianna as his girlfriend, Callie as his buddy. He loved them both, and maybe it had never occurred to him he didn't love Julianna the way a man should love his wife. If he had loved her that way, then he'd be as devastated as his grandmother assumed he was — as devastated as everyone assumed he was.

And suddenly, because he wasn't as devastated, because he realized he'd almost married someone he loved as a friend but not the way a man should love a wife, because suddenly he doubted he'd ever have what his grandparents, parents, and sister Vancy had, Noah felt depressed.

More depressed than he'd felt about his aborted wedding.

Rather than head out to the slopes, he spent the afternoon sitting in the chair, watching the snow fall, and mourning the life he'd thought he'd have and wondering where he went from here.

■ ■ ■ ■

Before she'd left for her day of beauty, Callie believed she had a vague notion of what spending a day at a spa entailed. And though she felt she had a more than adequate imagination, she quickly discovered it wasn't adequate enough for the reality of the experience.

In her fantasy spa dream, there had been dozens of beautiful women flitting about in soft silk robes that accentuated their every curve, being primped and pampered.

In reality, the halls were filled with very ordinary women — women you could meet in the grocery store, or even at Home Depot — looking as confused and as out of place as she felt. They all, Callie included, were walking around in big bulky terry robes that did a nice job of hiding any body flaws.

She was assigned a technician named Beatrice — "call me Bea" — who was old enough to have graduated high school at the same time as Nana Vancy. The woman was age-stooped and slight. She looked as if a stiff breeze would blow her over.

But as she had Callie drop her robe and crawl into a vat of mud, she took on all the bravado of a master drill sergeant.

"Half an hour," she barked as she set a timer and left the room.

Half an hour of sitting in mud?

It wasn't that Callie was averse to mud. Goodness knew, she spent enough time in it at work. Muddy construction zones were a fact of life. And there had been plenty of mud when she and Noah were younger, digging up earthworms for fishing while Julianna squealed in the background. Julianna had never been a fishing sort of girl and had even less use for worms.

A feeling of guilt stabbed her. She wasn't sure why thinking about her stepsister made her feel guilty, and she didn't have time to sort it out, because Bea, the drill sergeant, came back and ushered her out of the mud, into a shower, then on to the next torture session.

Bea took her for a body scrub, which on the surface didn't sound as bad as the mud, until Bea handed her a paper G-string and paper bra that managed to cover less than ten percent of her body. She had to figure out how to lie on the table and make the paper underwear cover the areas she'd like to cover. She wasn't sure she was overly successful, but Bea barely noticed as she proceeded to cover Callie in some gelatinous scrub thing, then place warm, wet towels all over her.

At first it wasn't overly unpleasant, but the room was not exactly warm, and the towels cooled rapidly. Callie was cold, covered in goo, and wearing soggy bits of paper that barely covered her girl parts.

The rest of the day was a blur. There was a wrap thing, a facial, manicure, pedicure. The pedicure was the worst of it. She was ticklish, and working at not twitching was tough.

Bea suggested waxing, but Callie put her pedicured foot down.

By the time she was led into the room for her massage, she wondered how any woman could handle this on a regular basis. Oh, bits of the day were nice, and she hoped that when everything was said and done, she'd look better, but, really, looking better couldn't be worth a whole day wasted.

That's when Bea introduced her to what a massage was. Muscles she didn't know she owned were kneaded and stretched until she almost groaned with pleasure. Oh, she probably could have done without the funky music and the smelly incense, but really, after an hour of Bea's tender mercies, she decided she'd go through another day at a spa as long as it ended in a massage.

"Thanks," she managed.

"You just stay on the table until you feel like moving. Your clothes are in the locker right across the hall."

It was five or so minutes later when Callie finally felt as if she could move, and she oozed off the table, slipped on her robe, and started across the hall to the changing room with her locker in it.

"Callie."

She turned, and there was Noah, also wearing a bathrobe. And he looked better in it than any of the women Callie had seen all day. His legs were bare, and though she knew she'd seen them before in the khaki shorts Noah wore during the summers, she was pretty sure that the white terry robe must set them off better, because, though she was sure she'd seen them, she'd never really noticed them.

But she was noticing them now.

If asked, Callie would never describe herself as leg woman. She was more of a kind-smile, killer-eyes woman. But Noah's legs, with their light sprinkling of hair covering sculpted muscles . . . well, they were nice.

Very nice.

Nice enough that they had her reconsidering her preferences. Nice enough to have her look up and check that, indeed, he did also have a kind smile and killer eyes.

And noticing that made her realize that Noah, her childhood friend, was gorgeous.

And noticing that made her feel nauseated.

This was Noah. A friend.

Nothing more.

"Callie? You okay?"

Desperately trying to think of a plausible excuse for her less-than-normal behavior, she blurted out, "Spa days turn your brain to mush."

He laughed. "Really?"

"I think it was the mud they stuck me in first thing. It didn't just leach the impurities out of my system, it leached the cells out of my brain, making coherent thought impossible."

Yes, that was a good explanation for her aberrant view of Noah Salo. Oh, once, for about a minute, she'd thought she had a crush on him, but that was years ago, and she was so over it. He was Noah, her friend. The guy she fished with. The guy she went to Home Depot with.

He was her buddy.

Her pal.

And pals did not notice other pal's legs.

Ever.

It was a rule somewhere, she was sure.

"So, why don't we go get dressed, and we'll go to dinner?"

"Food. Yes, food would be good. They fed me some toxin-leaching salad for lunch. I'm not sure the toxins leached anywhere, but if effectiveness is judged by taste, I'm going to live forever, because it was nasty."

"I'll feed you something guaranteed not to leach anything from you."

"And ice cream."

"It's the middle of winter. How on earth can you want ice cream?"

Callie sighed. "I'm so disappointed. I've spent years trying to train you, and still you forget that there's no such thing as a bad time for ice cream."

He laughed. "Sorry. I forgot. Ice cream, then."

"Try to remember it," she called as she hurried into her changing room, shut and locked the door, then collapsed against a wall.

Whatever that was, it was a momentary lapse, and after she was dressed and had some food in her, she'd forget it ever happened, she was sure. Because Noah, while he was the best friend a girl could want, would be horrible as anything more. He'd just been dumped, practically at the altar, by her stepsister. Definitely not a match made in heaven.

And Callie had just lost her boyfriend, not that she'd held out any hopes of ever marrying him.

Maybe the fact that she'd always expected her recent relationship to end meant she'd been unfair to him and to herself. After all, why date someone if you couldn't at least imagine spending the rest of your life with him?

And she couldn't with Jerry.

A sneaky little thought crept onto the threshold of her consciousness. Noah would be a perfect ever-after kind of guy. They liked the same things, were companionable. And if her reaction to his legs was any indication, she was attracted to him.

But even in her current mudded-and-beautified condition she couldn't imagine Noah's ever being attracted to her. He liked women like her stepsister. Julianna was feminine to the core. She'd never touched a worm, didn't know a dado saw from a miter saw. Julianna liked spa days and dresses. That was the kind of woman Noah Salo was attracted to.

Suddenly, despite the fact that she'd never wanted Noah to be attracted to her, Callie felt depressed.

Ice cream, she thought, trying to cheer

herself up.

But even ice cream couldn't lighten the weird funk she suddenly found herself in.

She dressed and tried to figure out what was wrong with her. It wasn't as if she'd want Noah to be attracted to her.

No, not at all.

That would be too weird.

CHAPTER FIVE

Noah had heard the expression *jaw-dropping,* but he'd never experienced the phenomenon before today. But now that he had, he had a new appreciation for other people's jaw-dropping moments.

Yes, his jaw hung practically against his chest as he watched Callie Smith come into the main room of the cottage. He knew it had to be Callie. He'd seen her go down the hall to her bedroom looking the same as ever. Despite her day at the spa and the way her hair was almost behaving, she'd still looked like Callie, wearing a pair of well-worn jeans and a bulky sweater.

And now, half an hour later, she'd come back totally different.

She had on a black dress and heels. She even had on jewelry. For the life of him, he couldn't remember ever seeing her wear jewelry before. But here she was, wearing a silver necklace, matching bracelet, and dangly earrings.

"Is there a problem?" She smoothed her dress down nervously.

Wanting to reassure her, he forced his jaw back into its normal position and smiled. "You look lovely."

"Thanks. Are you ready? I'm starving. And someone promised me ice cream."

"Okay, you might look all fancied up, but it's reassuring to know that my Callie's still there under all that makeup and stuff."

"I'm not your Callie," she said with a frown. "I'm my own woman."

"Wow, spa days make you testy." He grinned, hoping to counter her frown. "You know that's not what I meant."

He was relieved when she smiled back. "You're right — spa-ing makes me testy. Ice cream can only improve my mood."

"Then let's go to dinner."

A very big part of him wanted to help her on with her coat, but, given her reaction moments ago, no way was he going to risk it. He also didn't hold the door for her at their cottage or at the inn's main lobby, and he was relieved when the maître d' at the restaurant pulled out her chair for her and lived to tell the story.

"So, tell me about your day," he said, after their food was ordered and the wine steward had snootily brought over a bottle of red wine.

"Are you sure you want to risk it? My testiness might reassert itself."

"I'm hoping that talking about it will help you get over the trauma of the spa."

"I don't know if anything will. Noah, you should have seen what they did . . ."

She launched into a hilarious account of her day of horrors. He started laughing and was relieved when she joined in.

". . . but I have to say, the massage at the end made the rest of it almost worthwhile."

"I'd never had one before, but it wasn't half bad."

"Not half bad?" She sighed with utter contentment. "It was nirvana. It almost made the other stuff worth it."

"Almost?"

She laughed and reiterated, "Almost."

"So, what do we want to do tomorrow? It doesn't really matter to me," he said. And he realized it was true. It didn't matter what they did as long as he was doing it with Callie.

He'd even go shopping, and shopping was the type of excursion designed to torture a man. But he'd have done it willingly, as long as Callie kept smiling the way she was now.

As he listened to her chatting about possible activities for the next day, he realized he'd never really noticed how beautiful she was. It had nothing to do with her spa day and everything to do with Callie herself. She'd always been just a friend, and he'd have been hard pressed to describe her accurately if asked. But something had changed, and he was seeing her in a whole new light.

And he liked what he saw.

The next day was too cold for skiing. The sky was gray and ominous, and the snowfall was heavy. Noah had spent his morning trying not to trip over Callie — and trying to forget what she looked like in that big, bulky robe. It wasn't a robe designed to look sexy. He knew that. It was probably as asexual as a robe could get. And yet, on Callie, it looked good.

Very good.

Very, very good.

Which is why all morning his thoughts had drifted to Callie in that robe. It didn't matter that she was now wearing jeans and a bulky brown turtleneck, along with big brown slippers. All he could see was her in that robe.

If they spent any more time in here together, he was going to lose his mind. "What about a movie?"

"Pardon?"

"Let's get out of here," he said, suddenly sure that going out in public would help him shake the mental images of Callie that had kept him wide awake all night. "Let's head to the theater and make a deal to see whatever the next show is. Chick flick, action, horror, comedy . . . whatever's playing next."

She grinned. "You'll buy the big bucket of popcorn?"

"You buy the soda."

"You're on. Just let me grab my coat." Callie was ready in short order, and they drove to the theater.

It had been his idea, so Noah couldn't really complain when the next show at the small theater was a chick flick.

It wasn't a bad movie actually, not that he'd admit to having enjoyed it. He wasn't an expert at girly movies, but he was pretty sure it was a standard plot. Boy and girl meet, life gets in the way and they separate, and at the end they overcome their obstacles and get back together.

He couldn't help smiling as he glanced over at Callie, who was trying to wipe away tears without his seeing.

"You're crying," he whispered.

"Am not."

"Shh!" the old lady in front of them shushed.

Callie continued to wipe her cheeks even more furtively for the last ten minutes.

The house lights went up, and Noah stood.

"Not yet." Callie was firmly planted, staring at the screen as if waiting for the couple to kiss again.

Noah sat back down. "What are we watching for?"

"You know I never leave until the credits finish rolling."

He thought back and realized that even when they watched a DVD at home, she always waited for the credits to finish before turning it off.

"I've noticed, but I never asked why." Watching credits had to be the most boring thing Noah could think of. "Seriously, why?"

"See that?" She pointed to the screen. "The key grip's name is James McDonald."

"So?"

"When I see that the grip is James McDonald, I don't just see a name. I see his mother, agonizing over what to call the bald, dimpled child she's just given birth to. He was ugly. Most babies are. But he was hers, and that made him beautiful. She watched him grow from a bald little Yoda-looking baby into a tall, handsome man. And watching these credits roll by with his name — the name she gave him, the son she'd raised — she feels such incredible pride. *That's my Jimmy,* she thinks. That's why I wait. Maybe someday little Jimmy McDonald's mother will be watching the credits in the same theater, and she'll be so thrilled to have someone to share that pride with. *'That's my boy,'* she'll say. Pride and love. I stay to see it."

"How is it I never knew that?"

"Probably you were always so busy with Julianna, you never bothered to wonder."

"What other secrets do you have that I don't know, Callie?"

"No secrets."

"But things I don't know?" he pressed.

"Probably too many to be counted. You've always been my friend, Noah, but our friendship circled around Julianna, and when I'm next to her, I sort of fade away. I've never minded," she hastened to add. "I don't need the spotlight. But when we went to the movies, Julianna was there too, and she was where you focused, not on me and my weird little foible."

"I'm noticing now," he said, meaning it.

He was noticing a lot of things about Callie. He was seeing her as more than just a pal, a fishing buddy, a coworker. More than just a good friend.

He wasn't sure what to make about all he was seeing.

The last credit rolled by, and Callie stood. "Okay, we can go now."

"I don't think Jimmy's mom was in the audience today," he said, surveying the now empty theater.

"That's okay, maybe she'll be next time. Now, where are we going for dinner?"

"You just ate a huge tub of popcorn."

"You helped."

"Yeah, but you still ate a ton. You're really hungry?"

"Yep. But let's skip fancy. I mean, I'm not saying the restaurant at the hotel isn't nice, but we're not exactly dressed for it, and there was that strip of fast-food joints right on our way into the movie."

"And because you're hungry, close is good."

"It's not just the proximity. I really could go for a hamburger."

"Now you're talking." He laughed. He wasn't sure why. It was just that he was enjoying the afternoon. Enjoying Callie.

They laughed through a dinner of burgers

and fries, followed by the biggest sundaes Noah had ever seen.

"Where do you put it?" he asked as they drove back to the inn.

"Pardon?"

"All that food. Popcorn, a hamburger, and that sundae? I couldn't finish half of mine."

"I am a woman of many mysteries. And how I'm able to eat that much food is just one of the smaller mysteries."

"Hmm . . . What other mysteries do you have?"

She scrunched up her face in a way he suspected was supposed to look intimidating, but in the end she just looked cute.

"Now, if I told you," she said in a guttural voice, "I'd have to kill you."

"So what are we going to do tonight?" he asked as they walked back to the car.

"Poker."

He wasn't sure what he'd thought she'd say, but that wasn't on the list. "Poker?"

"The last time we played, you won. I want a chance to get even."

"Poker it is, at least if I can find a deck of cards. I'll ask at the desk." He walked to her side of the car and opened her door.

She looked surprised by the courtesy. "I can open my own door."

She seemed annoyed, and he wasn't sure

why. "Sorry. Blame Nana Vancy. She always taught me to open a date's door."

"I'm not a date. I'm a friend. And I'm betting you don't open the door for Matt."

He laughed as he walked to his side of the car and got in. "No. My brother-in-law is capable of opening doors for himself."

"Me too. And you don't have to bother asking for cards at the desk. I packed some, along with chips."

"You planned this?"

"Yes." She had that particular smile that said she was extremely pleased with herself.

He turned and eyed her suspiciously. "What are you up to?"

"Up to?" she asked, the picture of innocence, and she laughed, making him even more suspicious that somehow this was a setup of some kind.

When they got back to the cottage, it didn't take more than a couple of hands for him to realize Callie was taking the game very seriously.

Noah had never realized just how much Callie didn't like to lose. She studied her cards as intensely as if she were cramming for a test. Her brow would pucker, forming the cutest little wrinkle on the bridge of her nose. Her expressions should have made it easy to gauge her hands. Problem was, her nose wrinkled and her brow puckered, good hand or bad. She grimaced, tsked, and generally made a show of it, regardless of the quality of her cards.

Midway through the game, his stack of chips grew much lighter, he gave up trying to read her and tried to salvage his pride and win at least a few hands.

Two hours into the game he admitted defeat. "That's it. You win."

Callie crowed her victory. "I love poker."

"When did you get this good?"

"I've been playing in a monthly game with some of the guys from the crew."

"And do you win there?"

"Yes. I have quite the reputation as a poker ace."

"You know, Calista Smith, you're not the most gracious winner."

She shrugged, looking thoroughly pleased with herself and completely unrepentant. "I know. It's a curse."

He chuckled. "Well, next time I pick the game."

"I don't know if that will help you out. I win at most of them."

"Do you play Sudoku?"

"Huh?"

From her confused look, he knew he had her. "Well, I'll buy a couple of books, and that'll be our game tomorrow night. I'm afraid it'll be hard to see the mighty stumble, but somehow I'll survive witnessing your fall."

"Who's being cocky now?" It was Callie's turn to laugh. She couldn't remember when she'd spent a more enjoyable evening, but she knew it was getting late. "We'll just see tomorrow who's cocky and who's the winner. But for now I think I'm hitting the hay."

Noah glanced at the clock. "You're right. It's late. And if we want to hit the slopes early, we'd best get to bed."

He started to follow her down the hall.

"I can find my way on my own," she said a little testily.

"You forget, I'm heading to bed too, and my room's right next to yours."

His first inclination had been to walk her all the way to her door, but instead, he stopped at his own. "Well, good night."

"Night, Noah. And thanks for such a lovely day."

It had been a lovely day, she realized as she hurried into her room and shut the door. She hadn't thought about Jerry all day. And Noah hadn't seemed broken up over Julianna.

This trip had been good for both of them.

She was glad she'd come, she assured

herself as she got ready for bed.

Two sleepless hours later, she wasn't quite so glad.

Through the very thin wall she could hear Noah tossing and turning.

She wondered if he was thinking about Julianna and remembering that this was supposed to be his honeymoon. And thinking about his remembering his wedding that wasn't, about his wishing it was Julianna here with him instead of her, bothered her.

Noah was up early the next day, feeling bleary-eyed and tired.

He'd hardly slept. Callie had tossed and turned all night.

He wondered if she was thinking about Jerry. He had the coffee perking when she wandered into the kitchen. "You look like hell."

"Right back at you," she grumbled.

"Bad night?" he asked, though he didn't need to.

She shrugged. "You?"

He shrugged.

They both poured their coffees and sat staring at their respective mugs.

"How soon do you want to leave for the slopes?" he asked after about half a mug.

"Give me a few minutes."

She seemed distant today.

He decided he'd do his best to see to it that she didn't have time to think about Jerry again that week.

Chapter Six

"It's been a great week. I can't believe it's our last night," Noah said. "Thanks for that, Callie."

"You don't have to thank me. You did just as much to distract me from my own problems."

It had been a great week, despite the fact that they'd both just been jilted. Skiing, great meals, more poker, and Callie had learned to play Sudoku. She'd lost the first few days, but tonight she'd won, and not on just an easy puzzle but on a medium.

They were sitting on the couch, a fire going, and Noah seemed as reluctant to go to bed as she was. Callie didn't want the day to end, but even more she didn't want the night to begin. Because despite how wonderful the days had been, the nights had been long — very, very long. And she dreaded going to bed.

Each sleepless night had seemed to last a little longer than the one before.

"So, do you feel better?" Noah asked.

She thought about it a moment, and though she was tired, she did feel better. She nodded, realizing she was almost feeling too much better. "You?"

"Much. I've realized over this last week that Julianna may have done her and me both a big favor. Don't get me wrong — I love her — but maybe it's not the kind of love to build a relationship with. She's a friend — maybe friend enough to realize it before me and save us both from a big mistake. We didn't fit."

"What do you mean?" From where Callie sat, it had always looked as if they fit together just fine.

"Well, I tried to tell myself that coming to Maple Grove Inn was a great compromise between our tastes. Outdoor activities for me, pampering for her. But you and I both know, despite the great spa, she'd have hated it here. She wouldn't have wanted to ski, and she was never too keen on just sitting quietly and reading. She'd have been stir-crazy within two days."

"Maybe not," Callie said, though she didn't believe it. Julianna would have hated the rustic cabin and the skiing.

"Callie?" He looked at her, sensing her lie.

"Okay," Callie admitted, "so she'd have hated it. But she would have loved being with you."

He shook his head. "Do you realize how many things she and I don't have in common?"

"They say opposites attract."

He shook his head. "Come on, there has to be some give and take. But I wasn't willing to give enough to plan a honeymoon that didn't accommodate me."

"That's not selfish, just sensible. You can't give up who you are to make someone else happy."

"I think that's what ultimately would have happened. We'd both have given up huge parts of ourselves, and neither of us would have been the richer for it."

"So, now what do you do?" She pulled the quilt off the back of the couch and covered her legs with it.

"For starters, when I get home, I'm sending her a dozen roses . . . whatever color's for friendship. Pink, you think? Doesn't matter. I'll ask. And I'll send them with a card, thanking her for saving us."

"Then?"

He shrugged. "Get on with my life, I

guess. You?"

"Same thing." She pulled the quilt a little closer.

He raised his glass. "To getting on with our lives."

They clinked glasses and sipped their colas.

"How about, to new beginnings?" Callie asked.

They clicked glasses again.

"So, what about you?" he asked. "What are you going to do?"

She set her glass down on the coffee table slowly, giving herself time to collect her thoughts. "I'm going to find the right man."

"Who would that be?"

Her image of that perfect man came together immediately. "He's someone who likes the outdoors. All the stuff we do together — skiing, fishing, hiking." She paused and thought a moment, then added, "And I want a guy who knows how to be independent of me. Who isn't looking for a little woman, someone to follow him around and pick up after him. I'm not good at playing little woman."

"Me, either," he said seriously.

She laughed. "Glad to hear it. I have trouble picturing you as anyone's little woman. I guess my perfect man is someone who's a friend first, like you and I are. Not that I'm saying you and I . . ." She paused, desperately trying to find a way to undo those words, and finally gave up. "You know what I mean. A man like you who's not you."

"Thanks, I guess. But I think that was the most backhanded compliment I ever heard."

"Some days you just have to take what you can get."

"Here's to my finding a woman who's like you but not you, and to your finding a man like me who's not me."

"To us," she echoed, trying to laugh the conversation off as a joke but not feeling as if it was overly funny. Not funny at all.

It was their last night together, Noah realized as he listened to Callie toss and turn through the thin wall. He was going to miss having her next door. Miss being with her every day.

He thought about their dinner conversation, about what they wanted in their perfect boyfriend/girlfriend. He wanted someone who got him, who liked the same things. He'd find someone like that.

Someone like Callie, but not Callie.

And suddenly he wondered, why not Callie?

He loved her as a friend. He had ever since that first weekend she came to stay with her father and his new family. They enjoyed the same things, had always gotten along great. And he loved her passion for helping people. She'd worked for his family since her teen years, and she now used what she'd learned at Salo in a way that benefitted the whole community, one family at a time.

He remembered how she'd sat through the film credits, watching all those names go by and waiting for the day the key grip's mom was in the theater.

How had he never noticed that before? he wondered again.

And if he hadn't noticed that, how many other things had he missed?

He'd had a week with Callie and didn't feel as if he knew nearly enough.

But he realized he'd have time when they got home.

All the time in the world to discover everything he could about Calista Smith.

Something was wrong with Noah, Callie realized as they made the hour-long car ride home. He kept glancing at her, giving her the oddest looks.

She'd been feeling down about coming

home, but Noah's odd mood had her feeling on edge and made the sight of her small house most welcome.

"Well, thanks again," she said as they pulled into her driveway. "It was a wonderful time."

"I hope it helped you get over Jerry."

"Who?" she teased.

He grinned, and for a moment he was just Noah again. But as he smiled at her, he got that same funny look on his face.

"What on earth is wrong with you?"

"What do you mean?"

"The looks."

"What looks?"

She wanted to scream in frustration but decided distance would be the best cure for whatever was bothering them both. Noah and his odd looks, her and her odd thoughts about him.

"Never mind. I just want to thank you again."

"Same here. Thank you."

At a loss for what to do next, she decided to simply end the sudden awkwardness. "I'd better go. I know I've got a mountain of work to make up because of last week. I'll talk to you soon."

And before he could say anything or look at her again, she got out, opened the back door, grabbed her suitcase and her ski bag, then hurried into the house.

She glanced over her shoulder, and he was still just sitting there, watching her.

She hurried inside and made herself a promise. She was not going to think about Noah Salo. She was going to avoid him.

And she was going to get over whatever weird emotional aberration was causing her uncharacteristic thoughts about him.

From this moment on, she was on a man hiatus. She was going to take some time off from dating and figure out exactly what she was looking for. What kind of man she wanted.

But even as she had the thought, a picture formed in her mind.

A picture of Noah Salo.

The house felt too empty, Noah realized after he'd unpacked. Even though they'd just gotten home, Noah wondered if he should call Callie and see if she wanted to do dinner.

He spent a good ten minutes looking for the phone before he realized he'd placed it on the charger, which was generally the last place he'd look for it. But before he could dial, the doorbell rang.

He tossed the phone onto the couch and

hurried to the door. Maybe Callie had come over to invite him to dinner.

"Hey . . ." His greeting faded when, instead of Callie, he found his grandmother, bearing a towering stack of plastic dishware. "Nana."

"I came with food, like I promised. Dori said you told her you were coming home today, and I started cooking."

He was going to kill his little sister. The nice thing about his older sister, Vancy's, new marriage was that she didn't have time to run tattling to Nana and the rest of his family about him.

"Nana, I said I'm fine."

She juggled her dishes in one hand and patted his cheek with the other. "You're putting on a good front, but I know you're not fine. We all know you're not."

"We?" he asked, dreading her response.

"I called the family over for dinner, so we all can comfort you."

"Oh."

"After being destroyed by my curse, you need a lot of comforting." She started toward his kitchen, then spun around and said, "Make yourself useful. Go to my car and get another load of food."

"There's more?"

"Of course. You can't have a family dinner

without plenty of food."

He did as he was told and brought another mountain of plastic containers into the kitchen. "Who all is coming?"

"Everyone." His grandmother opened a lid, sniffed whatever the bowl contained, then rummaged for a spoon in his drawer and stirred it. "Let's see, there's your mom and dad, your grandfather, Vancy, Matt and the twins, and Dori."

"You know, I was sort of looking forward to having a quiet night," he tried, though he knew it was useless.

"Quiet?" She shook her head. "No, what you need is your family around you during times of crisis. We gave you a few quiet weeks, but that's all over now. We're not going to let you wallow by yourself in your pain. You're going to be surrounded by the warmth of your family until we're sure you're totally over your crushing loss."

He knew he had to explain that *crushing* wasn't the right description for his loss. "Nana, I —"

"Hush. That's all I want to hear from you on this matter. You need us, and the Salos might not be known for their weddings, but we have never let a family member down, *kedvenc.*"

After that, there was nothing left for it.

They came in dribbles. First his sister Vancy, her husband, Matt Wilde, and the five-year-old twins, Rick and Chris. Vancy, his grandmother's namesake, hugged him. "I know how hard this is, but you'll get through it. Julianna wasn't the right one, but you'll find the woman who is. I just know it."

"I'm really doing much better than any of you think."

"Yes, that's what you would say, but, Noah, you don't have to be strong for us. We're here for you." She sounded like his grandmother, but before he could inform her of that fact, his parents pulled into his drive. So he left the door open and waited for the inevitable.

"Noah!" his mother gushed as she wrapped him in yet another hug.

His father patted his back. "It'll be fine, son." Then, looking extremely uncomfortable with all the emotions, he hurried off to play with Rick and Chris.

"Mom, really, I'm fine."

"Oh, you were always such a brave boy. Do you remember that time you and Callie decided to go sledding down by Four Mile Creek, and your sled hit the tree? You came home without your front tooth, with a gash bleeding profusely, and do you know what

109

you said to me?"

"Mom, really, I'm fine?" He didn't really remember, but it wasn't too hard to guess.

His mom nodded. "Ever since then, I've ignored your protests."

"But this time —"

"This time the whole family is going to comfort you. You've had your time to brood. Now we're going to help you recover." She finally let him go. "Let me go check on your grandmother."

Noah was about to close the front door again, but Dori's Land Rover pulled into the drive. With her long legs, Dori never really walked; she strode to the front door. Rather than hugging or gushing, she just looked at him. "You don't look half bad."

"I'm fine."

"Good." She slapped his back, much as his father had done, and walked into the house.

Noah finally shut the door, but he hadn't gone more than a couple of steps when someone else rang the doorbell. Mentally he tallied up the family already present and knew before he opened the door that he'd find Bela Salo on the other side.

His grandfather, a giant bear of a man, sauntered into the hallway. "You look fine."

"Finally, someone who realizes I'm okay.

It's been three weeks, and —"

"Well, make sure your grandmother understands you're okay, because she's making my life a misery. All those accusing stares, telling me it's my fault for missing our wedding, which made her say those words and curse the whole family. I'm telling you, a man can only take so much. You make sure she knows you're all right and that this isn't my fault."

"I'll do my best, Papa, but you know Nana."

"I do," he admitted. "I've been married to her enough years to know she's become obsessed with this curse thing. You or Dori had better break it, because she'll be after poor Chris and Rick next if you don't. Do you want to be responsible for your nephews going through this?"

"No, sir."

"Then fix it."

Noah wasn't quite sure what his grandfather expected him to do, but he'd agree to anything to get the door closed and get out of the hallway.

His grandfather eyed him a moment, then nodded and headed toward the sound of the boys laughing in the living room. "Where are my great-grandsons?" he bellowed, which led to more shrieks from the boys.

Noah knew his family meant well, but their outpouring of sympathy made him feel like a fraud. He knew he wasn't suffering the way they thought he was.

He wished he was back at the Maple Grove Inn with Callie. Being with her had been simple and fun. More than that, being with her had made him feel good. Feel right. And he wondered again how he hadn't noticed or appreciated that about Callie before.

He'd hated saying good-bye to her and wished they'd gone out to dinner and he'd missed this impromptu family reunion, or that she was here now.

And why shouldn't she be?

Feeling James Bondish, with his plan in place, he went into the living room, where his grandfather was playing with the boys, and picked up the phone.

"Noah, what are you doing?" his grandfather asked.

"Just got to make a quick business call. Go on with your game."

He hurried to his bedroom, shut the door, and dialed Callie's number.

"This is Callie. Well, not really Callie, but rather her machine. You know what to do."
Beep.

"Callie, it's Noah. I know I just dropped you off, but I wondered if you'd like to come over to my place for dinner. And before you start protesting that it's not necessary, I'll agree, it's not necessary for you, but I've got a house filled with family, all intent on comforting me. I could use your help convincing them I'm all right. If you can make it, I'd appreciate it."

He hung up.

"Noah, honey," his mother called through the closed door, "we'll be eating in a bit."

"I just had to make a business call, Mom. I'll be right out."

Knowing there was nothing left for it, he went out to face his family. The family bound and determined to comfort him, whether he needed it or not.

As she'd unpacked from the trip, Callie decided it would be in her best interest to steer clear of Noah Salo for a while. She'd had too many unusual thoughts about him for comfort. Add to that the odd looks he'd kept shooting her way, and she was sure they just needed some distance now.

She'd made her mind up that they'd both been dumped and she'd simply mistaken gratitude for his friendship for something more. She'd give him a bit of distance, and everything would settle back into place — she was sure of it.

Maybe that's what his weird looks had been about. He'd realized she was harboring a-bit-more-than-friendliness feelings for him and was worried about it. He would probably be glad to keep some space between them.

When she heard his voice on her machine, she told herself firmly not to go.

Unfortunately, listening to good advice had never been her strong suit, which was why she found herself pulling into Noah's driveway to rescue him from his loving family.

She got out of the car and walked up to the front door.

She should turn around without knocking or ringing the bell. She should just leave Noah to his family's loving attention and go home and take a bubble bath. And so she knocked.

One of the twins — she still had trouble telling them apart — opened the door. "Hey, Callie."

"Hi —"

She was saved from guessing a name when the twin screamed, "Uncle Noah, Callie's here!"

"Come on in," whichever twin it was

told her.

"I can't stay," she said.

"Okay." He slammed the door in her face, and Callie was left standing on the snow-covered porch, wishing she'd asked to wait in the foyer.

The door opened, and Noah smiled. "What are you doing out there?"

"Waiting for you."

"Come in. You didn't have to knock. After all, we've shared a house for a week. I think that gives you certain rights, and stepping into my foyer without my specific invitation is one of them." He ushered her inside and shut the door. "Take your coat off."

She didn't take off her coat, because now that she was here, she was thinking better about staying. Looking at Noah was enough to make her stomach twist, not in an I'm-going-to-be-sick way but in an ooh-la-la sort of way. And she'd never been an ooh-la-la sort of woman.

Noah's rumpled dark hair made her fingers itch to smooth it. And thinking about running her fingers through his hair had her heart racing in a pleasant sort of way. Well, it would be pleasant if she were fantasizing about anyone but Noah Salo.

No, she was going to pretend she hadn't picked up his message and just leave.

"I was in the neighborhood, running some errands, and I brought you this." She reached into her bag and pulled out a manila folder. "It's the specs and estimates on that new house HOMEs has bought. You said Salo's might be willing to help us on one, and I thought this one might be a good choice."

"Great." He took the folder. "But come in and stay for dinner. Nana's been cooking. I left a message on your answering machine inviting you."

"Didn't get it," she lied, crossing her fingers behind her back. "And I should be going."

"Stay."

"It's a family thing. I don't want to intrude."

He lowered his voice and said, "Rescue me from my family. They think I need to be comforted, and they're bound and determined to see to it, whether I want it or need it."

"Really, Noah, we just spent a week together. You've got to be sick of me by now."

"Callie, I'll never be sick of you."

She snorted. "I hope you've got better lines than that for women, because that was truly lame, Salo."

"But you're going to stay, right?"

She sighed, trying to convince him she felt put-upon instead of elated at the idea of spending more time with him. "Fine. I'll stay. But you're going to owe me big. You know Nana Vancy will try to fix me up with someone, just like she does every time I see her. *'Callie,* kedvenc, *you need a man. A good man like my Bela or my son Emil. You'd make some man a wonderful wife.'*

"And then I'll say something about how I'd rather find a man who will make me a wonderful husband, and then she'll laugh and set me up with someone."

"Chicken," he said with a laugh.

"Last time I let her fix me up . . . well, let's just say if we were in an arm wrestling match, I'd've won hands down."

"Hey, as long as she only fixes you up with men you can take, it's all right. And now you *have* to come in because I need to prove I could take you in an arm wrestling match."

"That was just a figure of speech."

"Yeah, but you've got me feeling as if I need to prove my manhood."

"And now that you've said that, how on earth could I beat you, knowing I'd have you questioning your very manhood? I'd have to throw the match, and that would leave you feeling even worse."

"My manhood could take it. Come on, you know that once Nana spots you there's no escape."

"That's why I'd better go —"

As if on cue, Noah's grandmother looked around the corner into the foyer. "Callie, *kedvenc,* take off your coat and boots and come in. We're almost ready to sit down to dinner."

"Really, I just dropped off some papers for Noah."

"Lucky for us, because now we'll have the pleasure of your company at dinner." She turned back into the kitchen, where they could hear her announce, "Get another setting. Callie's here."

"You're stuck now," Noah said, grinning.

"If I didn't know any better, I'd think you planned that."

He laughed and led her into the kitchen.

Callie remembered that when Noah built the house, he'd been specific about needing a huge kitchen. Knowing he didn't do much cooking, Callie had questioned him. He'd grinned and told her that his grandmother would never forgive him if he had a tiny one.

And his kitchen, which normally looked big, was now crowded with Salos.

"Callie!" was their cry in unison as she

followed Noah into the room.

"Have a seat by me." Noah's grandfather patted a chair at the big table where all the adults were crowded. The boys were sitting on stools at Noah's kitchen island. "Tell me about HOMEs. Any new projects?"

"As a matter of fact, I just brought Noah . . ."

Noah watched as Callie laughed in a corner with Dori. He was pretty sure they'd formed an alliance, running interference for each other with his grandmother.

Callie felt at home with his family in a way Julianna never had.

Thinking about his ex-fiancée didn't bring any pain. All he felt was a pang of nostalgia for their seemingly carefree past. That sounded clichéd, even in his mind, but there it was.

"Earth calling Noah."

His older sister, Vancy, was standing next to him. "How're things?" he asked her.

"I'm fine. But how about you?"

"Better than the family seems to think I am."

She laughed. "If Nana Vancy thinks you're hurting, then the whole family has no choice but to come comfort you with her. Look at it this way: you might not need the comforting, but at least you get dinner."

"Nana did bring dumplings." They were his favorites.

"Well, there you have it. I'd pretend to suffer in order to get the dumplings. She's tried to teach me to make them, but mine never taste even close." She stopped teasing, leaned forward, and kissed his cheek. "You'll find the woman you were meant for. I believe that."

"I was thinking I'd be the boys' bachelor uncle. I could dote on them."

"I don't think that's your future."

"Dinner!" their grandmother called.

Noah found himself sitting next to Callie, and he leaned over and whispered, "Thanks for staying."

She smelled good. Not a flowery, girly sort of smell, but rather a fresh-air, hint-of-spice sort of scent. It made him want to lean closer and bury his face in her neck.

More than that, he wanted to pull her into his arms and kiss her.

When that realization hit, he pulled away from Callie and sat firmly in his own personal space.

She smiled and mouthed the words, *You're welcome.*

His grandmother stood and cleared her throat.

For a moment Noah worried she was going to say something about him. Instead she simply said, "I believe Vancy and Matt have something to share with you all."

The couple stood. Matt took Vancy's hand and nodded to her. Vancy smiled up at him, and Noah felt another pang at the connection he saw between them. That's what had been missing with him and Julianna. And he realized he wanted that. He wanted someone who looked at him the way Vancy looked at Matt, someone he'd look at the way Matt looked at Vancy.

"We were going to hold off a while, but we decided that this impromptu family meal was the right place to announce that Matt and I are going to have a baby in August."

There was an uproar. His mom and grandmother both began crying, and then his father and grandfather were slapping Matt's back as if he were the first man in history to discover how to make a baby.

That's when he noticed Chris and Rick sitting quietly on their stools and looking a lot less enthusiastic than the others.

Noah got up and walked over to their seats. "Problem, boys?"

"Uncle Noah, when the baby comes, what will we be to him?" Rick asked.

"What?"

"Aunt Vancy and Uncle Matt are our aunt and uncle. But they're sort of like our mom and dad, since we ain't got none," Chris said.

"We do got one — we got a dad — but he don't want us, so we live with Uncle Matt, and he's like our dad."

"And our dad's like our uncle," Chris added.

"So what's this kid going to be to us?" Rick asked.

"This baby — well, he or she" — Noah made sure to include the possibility of the baby's being a girl — "will be your cousin. But you know, the baby is going to think of you two as if you were brothers."

"Do you think Uncle Matt and Aunt Vancy would let us call him our brother?" Chris asked softly.

"Is that what you want to call him?"

The two dark-haired heads bobbed up and down.

"Then I think you should ask Uncle Matt and Aunt Vancy, but I'm betting they'll think it's a wonderful idea."

"See? I told you," said Chris. "That baby's going to need big brothers. And we need a little brother."

"Uh, boys," Noah said, interrupting the potential fight with a reality check, since the boys hadn't noticed his first mention of a girl. "I hate to bring this up, but you do realize that the baby might not be a boy, right?"

Two sets of eyes bored into him with shock.

Noah grinned. "You know, when Grandma was expecting Aunt Dori, I was sure she was going to be a boy. I told everyone I was going to have a little brother. When Mom came home with a girl, I was so mad."

"But Aunt Dori is almost as good as a boy," Chris assured him.

"Hey, I heard that, squirt," Dori said as she came up behind them. "I'll have you know, girls are way better than boys."

Chris and Ricky both laughed.

"Hey, I mean it," Dori insisted.

"Mean what?" Callie asked as she came up behind them.

"The twins think I'm *almost* as good as a boy."

Callie was a bit more diplomatic. "Girls are just as good as boys. Neither is better than the other. When your Uncle Noah and I were kids, I did everything he did. I fished and skied and I *so* could out-climb him when it came to trees."

The boys looked at Noah, as if expecting him to deny Callie's climbing abilities.

"I'm afraid it's true. Callie was so tiny compared to me, she could go way higher in the trees."

"Well, if we have a sister . . ." Ricky said, then glanced nervously at Callie and Dori. When they didn't correct him and tell him the baby would be a cousin, he grinned and finished, "I guess we'll teach her to be just like a boy."

"There you go," Noah said.

"Hey, you two," Vancy said, coming up to the boys and wrapping them in a dual hug. "I'm so proud of you."

She looked up at everyone else. "They heard about the baby last night, because we felt they should know first. And they didn't spill the beans."

"What beans?" Ricky asked.

"It means, you didn't tell us the secret," Noah said.

"We keep secrets good." Chris' chest puffed out with pride.

"Aunt Vancy," Ricky said nervously, "Uncle Noah said we'll be almost like big brothers to the baby."

The boys both looked nervous again as they waited for Vancy's response. "This baby is going to be so lucky to have you two as big brothers." She kissed them both.

Matt came over and joined them. Noah

watched them and realized how much he wanted what they had. He looked at Callie, whose eyes met his, and he realized that when he looked at her, something in him stirred. Something he'd never felt before.

"Callie, *kedvenc,* I have this man I'd like you to meet. He's a landscaper who was working on Bela's new project, and I thought —"

"No, Nana. Callie doesn't want you setting her up." The words just came tumbling out of Noah's mouth. He knew he had no right to dictate whom Callie saw, but he wasn't about to aid and abet her finding a new man. He hastily added, "Dori doesn't either. We know you're worried about the curse, especially with a new generation of Salos on the way —"

"Of course, I'm worried. But —"

"No buts. Speaking for all the single Salos and their friends, we don't want to be set up. When we find love, it will be on our own terms."

"But, Noah —"

"I'm serious, Nana." He tried to assume the tone his grandfather took with his grandmother whenever he tried to reel her in. "No. Callie's too polite to say it herself, but she doesn't want to be set up."

"Noah, I think I'm capable of speaking

for myself with either you or your grandmother. I don't need a man doing my talking for me or stepping in to rescue me." She turned to his grandmother. "Nana, I'd be pleased to meet your man."

"*Kedvenc,* I simply wanted to tell you he might be someone interested in volunteering for the new HOMEs project Salo's is going to take on for you. But if you like, I can see if he's single and looking."

Noah watched as Callie turned a pretty shade of pink. "No, no. That's fine. I didn't really want to go on a blind date, but I didn't like your grandson's feeling he needed to save me. I don't need any man to save me."

"Well, far be it from me to try to help you out."

"What's going on?" Dori asked.

"Your brother was trying to play big he-man and save both of us poor, incapable women."

Noah could see Callie's annoyance and knew she was trying to find an ally.

"From what?" Dori asked.

"From me," Nana said. "He thought I was trying to set Callie up on a date, and he didn't like it. He said you could all find your own dates and I should back off in case my curse makes things worse." As she said the words, Nana's eyes narrowed, and she studied Noah in a way that made him feel decidedly uncomfortable.

"Noah, feel free to save me from that any time you want," Dori said. "Last time Nana set me up, he was practically geriatric."

"I am the grandmother and deserve a bit of respect," Nana huffed. "And Bernard was in his thirties. A nice, stable man."

"Stable financially, she means," Dori said. "But mentally? Not so much."

"Dora Lee Salo . . ." And their grandmother launched into a lecture about Dori's respecting her elders.

"I've got to go," Callie said suddenly. She stood, yelled a blanket "Good night" to everyone, and walked toward the front door, deserting poor Dori to her grandmother's lecture.

Noah didn't hesitate to abandon Dori as well as he hurried after Callie. He caught her at the front door. "Hey, are you mad?"

"No," she said unconvincingly. "I just have to leave. I didn't intend to stay."

He'd been around women long enough not to believe her denial. "I'm sorry I tried to save you. It won't happen again."

"That's not it, not at all. I just have to leave. I've got work to do. I took an unexpected week off, remember?"

"But —"

"No buts, remember?"

"Callie, could we meet for dinner tomorrow, or any night you say this week? I was going to call you tonight and ask you out, but then my family showed up with their cheer-up-Noah plans. I'd really like to go out tomorrow night. I need to talk to you." He threw that last part in, hoping it would soften her enough to make her say yes.

Instead of immediately agreeing, she hesitated and finally stuttered, "I, uh. I mean, well —"

"Please?"

Her expression softened. "Sure. Tomorrow's fine."

"I'll pick you up."

"You don't have to."

"I know. But it makes sense to drive together."

She nodded. "Thanks for dinner, Noah. And for looking over the specs for HOMEs."

He planned to just say good night and that she was welcome, but instead he found himself leaning down and kissing her. Kissing her as if he'd spent an eternity being deprived of her kisses and had to make up for lost time.

She pulled back and looked at him with a deer-in-the-headlights look. "Noah, what was that?"

"We'll talk tomorrow." He didn't mean to be cryptic, but he wasn't sure *what* that had been.

What he wanted it to be.

What it meant.

Maybe, given twenty-four hours, he could figure it out before they talked. "Good night, Callie."

She had her coat on and buttoned before he could say anything else. Not that he blamed her. He'd just changed the rules of their friendship. She was confused. But so was he.

They'd straighten it all out tomorrow.

CHAPTER SEVEN

Noah Salo had kissed her.

Callie spent a long night tossing and turning, replaying the kiss over and over. Trying to adjust to the fact that Noah had kissed her.

Even more, trying to adjust to the fact that she hadn't minded a bit.

It was that second part that was actually the biggest part of her sleepless night. Because Noah's kissing her wasn't her fault, but her not minding was.

She felt as if she'd betrayed her stepsister. Not that Julianna was engaged to, or even dating, Noah any longer. Still, for as long as she could remember, it had been Noah and Julianna.

Julianna and Noah.

Callie had been the interloper.

The hanger-onner.

The sidekick.

Finally at four, she made her bleary-eyed

way into the office, a small second-floor walk-up on Parade Street across from Nickel Plate Mills, which served as the office for HOMEs. The city had invested a lot of time and money renewing Parade Street, and Nickel Plate Mills was a prime example of how beautifully it was working. It was the perfect area for a business that wanted to not only give people homes but also to help renew the city.

Callie's very first job had been with Salo Construction, but even right out of school she'd known she wanted to do something more. She wanted to make a difference.

HOMEs was small. Noah's grandfather had helped her get the organization off the ground, but he left running it to her. Despite their lack of size, they'd already done a lot of good in the community. HOMEs bought run-down properties and, with the help of local businesses and banks and builders, renovated them, then sold them at only slightly over cost, making just enough of a profit to keep the business going. HOMEs' newest project was her twelfth house.

An even dozen.

She wished she'd gone to another firm to partner with her on the house, but at the time it had seemed fitting that she work with Salo Construction on it. The Salo family and their business were both such a big part of her life. But now, working with Noah on the new house had lost some of its appeal.

Not some.

All.

She needed to put distance between herself and him.

Maybe she could call and tell him another contractor had asked to participate. It would only be a little fib. It wouldn't hurt anyone.

"Callie?"

She jumped. She'd been so lost in thought, she hadn't heard anyone come into the office. Looking at her stepsister — tall, blond, and oh-so-perfectly beautiful, both inside and out — she felt a stab of guilt and wished almost anyone else had walked through the door.

She'd kissed Julianna's fiancé.

Well, Julianna's ex-fiancé.

It was wrong.

Very wrong.

"Callie, is something wrong?" Julianna asked, as if she could read Callie's mind.

"No. Nothing." Another lie.

Callie, who prided herself on her honesty, had contemplated and now actually lied, all in the span of two minutes.

"Callie," Julianna said gently.

It was that gentleness that was Callie's undoing.

"Don't be nice to me. I've betrayed you. Stabbed you in the back."

"Come sit down and take a deep breath. You're not making any sense."

Reluctantly, Callie sat on the very end of the couch, but Julianna didn't follow suit and sit on the other end; she sat right next to Callie. "Tell me."

"I went on your honeymoon with Noah," she blurted out. "He switched the honeymoon suite for a two-bedroom cabin, but the walls were thin, and I could hear every move he made. We spent the week skiing, seeing movies, and playing poker. I even went on your spa day."

"I'm trying to picture you at a spa and just can't get my brain to wrap around the concept of my little sister, Callie, spa-ing."

Julianna waited and looked disappointed when Callie couldn't even force a smile. But Callie just couldn't manage it, knowing that she'd kissed Noah.

"Callie," Julianna said again softly. "Going away with Noah wasn't betraying me. That was doing exactly what I asked you to do — look out for him."

"Yeah, I figured you'd be happy about

that, but then I messed it all up by kissing him. Well, not kissing him, but letting him kiss me." She waited, expecting Julianna to start raving about how she wished their parents had never met. How she hated the fact that she had such a duplicitous stepsister. How she never wanted to talk to Callie ever again.

Instead, Julianna burst out laughing. "Good for you."

"Huh?"

"Listen, I've told you over and over that I love Noah, but I wasn't in love with him. And I've always loved you as well. Why would I be upset that two people I love finally found out they were meant for each other? I figured it out at the stag, when I saw the two of you on the dance floor."

"Jules —" Oh, no. That was why Julianna had broken off the wedding plans.

"No. I was dancing with Darren, and I just knew that he and I . . . I knew that Noah and I couldn't . . ." Two incomplete sentences didn't stop Julianna from finishing, "But you and Noah? I can see it."

"You can't see anything. We just kissed. Well, he kissed me, and I didn't stop him right away."

"Again, good."

"Listen, Julianna. I betrayed you. You're supposed to be furious."

"You can't make it so by simply repeating it over and over. You didn't betray me, and I'm not furious. If you and Noah end up together, I'll be thrilled. The truth is, I'm seeing Darren."

"Darren?"

"Duffy. Darren Duffy. Noah's friend. I was dancing with him at the stag when I realized that I felt something for him. Afterward, Darren and I talked, and, well . . ." She shrugged. "I think I'm falling in love with him, and because of that, I realize even more than ever, what I felt for Noah wasn't the happily-ever-after sort of love, but more of the friends-since-childhood sort. And like I said, because I am his friend, I want him to be happy. I think you're the woman who could make him happy."

"Stop saying that. I'm not the woman for Noah."

"Why?"

"It would just be too weird. You two were an item for years. I'd always feel like second best."

"Did you feel like second best when he kissed you?"

"No." She paused, trying to sort out how she felt. "I felt confused."

"Confused good? Or confused not-so-good?"

"Let's stop talking about Noah. Tell me about Darren. I met him but don't know much about him."

Julianna launched into a Darren-fest. She talked about his love of the arts and their other shared interests. Mainly she talked about how he made her feel. Giddy, confused, happy . . .

Callie realized that those were the primary emotions she felt around Noah. Giddy, confused, happy. Plus a bit of scared.

". . . I think I love him," Julianna finished.

And that's where any similarities between Callie's feelings and Julianna's ended. Callie did not love Noah Salo.

Not at all.

Not even a little.

Well, maybe a little, if you counted loving him like a friend.

But no more than that. She wouldn't allow herself to let it be any more than that because . . .

Because of Julianna? No, obviously Julianna wasn't having a problem with the idea.

Because she worked for Salo Construction, and with Bela Salo at HOMEs? No. The family wouldn't mind, she was pretty sure.

Because? Because she was afraid. They were both getting over relationships, and they were too good of friends to spoil it by rebounding with each other.

Plus, given her track record, she didn't dare let things with Noah move beyond friendship, because she couldn't stand to lose him. And if they moved beyond friendship, she would lose him eventually. She lost all the guys she dated. She'd gotten along fine without all of them, but she'd be lost without Noah.

So, no. Anything more than friendship with Noah Salo was out of the question.

"I really am happy with Darren," Julianna said.

"Then I'm happy for you," she managed. But she wondered how Julianna could love any man more than Noah. This Darren sounded nice enough, but from what she remembered, he wasn't nearly as good-looking as Noah. She'd be the first to admit, though, that looks didn't matter nearly as much as other things.

Noah was inherently kind. Look how he'd offered to take her along on his honeymoon to help her get over her breakup with Jerry. She hardly felt a pang for her ex, because she'd known for a long time that they didn't have a future together. And if she were honest, she'd have to admit that she hadn't needed the trip with Noah to get over Jerry.

Yes, Noah was good-looking and kind. He was also hardworking and loyal.

He sounded like a Boy Scout.

She concentrated on Julianna. "All I want is for you to be happy, and if this Darren does that, well, then, I like him already."

"Same here. And I wish you'd give Noah a chance. You two would be perfect together."

Perfect?

With Noah Salo?

No way.

"I'm used to a quiet life. Except for the weekends I stayed with Dad, you, and your mom, life with my mom was subdued and reserved. That's what I'm used to — quiet and order. I can't ever imagine finding that with the Salo family."

"Come on, Callie, this is me. You can use all the excuses you want, but at least try to find one that I might believe. You love the Salos as much as I do."

"I love them, but that doesn't mean I love *him.*"

"Maybe you should."

"I like my life as it is." She changed the subject. She didn't want to fall for Noah.

Her track record with men was abysmal. They all ended up seeing her as a friend.

Noah had started out seeing her as a friend, and she didn't believe he'd be able to see her as anything more, despite the kiss.

And if he tried but couldn't manage? No, she couldn't risk it.

After Julianna left, Callie knew that Noah was still at work, so she called his house rather than his cell phone and left a message, canceling their dinner. Maybe it was cowardly, but she didn't want to talk to him. She wasn't sure he'd meant their dinner as a date, but she wasn't taking any chances.

She didn't want to date him. She wasn't willing to take that risk.

She was going to avoid Noah Salo until he'd gotten over whatever it was he was going through.

How hard could that be?

Noah showed up on Callie's doorstep two nights later. He'd been calling, leaving messages to no avail.

It didn't take a rocket scientist to realize Callie was avoiding him. And from there, it was no great mental leap to figure out why.

Noah wasn't going to allow a little thing like Callie's hiding to keep him from seeing her. Which was why he wasn't just standing on her porch, he was holding a pizza box, a DVD, and a file about her newest project.

He knocked on the door. "Callie, open up. I know you're in there. Your car's in the driveway."

He knocked again. "I'll just stay here all night, making noise and generally causing a commotion. I'm sure your neighbors will love that."

Another knock. "And if that doesn't work, I'll call Nana Vancy and tell her how worried I am that your car's in the driveway and you're not answering the door. She'll break in, and you won't even be able to call the police. I mean, you'd never have my grandmother arrested, would you? Of course not. Wouldn't it be better to just open up? I've got pizza. By my reckoning, you owe me a dinner."

He knocked again. "And I've got a movie that we can watch after we talk about your newest building renovation. I've got news. You wouldn't want to miss out on Salo Construction's assistance, would you?"

The door opened, and he carefully schooled his expression so he didn't appear to gloat. But he'd pretty much known that mentioning either Nana Vancy or the project would get him in.

"Sorry. I didn't hear you. I was in the

shower."

He did a slow once-over, noting she was fully dressed and her hair dry, then tilted his head and gave her *the look. The look* was one both his mother and grandmother frequently used on him to indicate a lack of belief.

Callie glanced down, then at him, and without a trace of embarrassment blatantly lied. "You've always said I dressed fast. Guess I proved you right."

"Are you going to let me in?"

She sighed. It was the sound of the truly put-upon. "I guess."

"Oh, be still, my heart. That kind of enthusiasm is such an ego booster."

"Your ego doesn't need any boosting."

"If I told you I got the pizza with every-thing but anchovies, would my company be more welcome?"

"Well, the pizza's company would." She smiled, softening the response, letting him know she was teasing. "Come on, let's take it to the kitchen, and you can show me your figures while we eat."

He followed her to the kitchen and set the pizza and files on the counter. "If I show you my figures, will you show me yours?"

She choked. "Pardon?"

"The figures for the project," he clarified

innocently. "What did you think I meant?"

She eyed him suspiciously. "I just didn't hear you, that's all."

"Like you didn't hear me at the door?"

She got two plates out of the cupboard, then opened the drawer for silverware. "I was getting dressed."

"I thought you were in the shower."

"I *was* in the shower." She set the items down on the counter. "But after I finished, I got dressed."

"Ah."

"What is wrong with you?" she asked.

"I don't know what you mean."

"You're not acting like yourself," she said, plopping napkins down next to the plates.

"I should have brought some wine to go with the pizza."

"No wine." She opened the fridge. "I have soda. Cola, lemon-lime . . ."

"Cola's fine."

She got two cans, set them on the counter as well, then took a seat on one of the stools and helped herself to a slice of pizza. "Now, what do you have for me?"

He followed suit, dishing up his plate, then answering, "I've talked to the crew, and I can give you two weeks' worth of a couple hours every evening with your volunteers. Looking at your job list, I'm thinking that should take care of most of it."

"Great. I've talked to Christopher's Plumbing, and they said they'd help."

"How about the electric?" he asked.

"I hadn't gotten that far."

"Let me talk to Johnson for you."

"That would be appreciated." She took a bite of the pizza and closed her eyes for a moment longer than it took for a blink. She looked totally enraptured with the taste.

Noah swallowed compulsively. "Uh, Callie?"

Her eyes popped open. "Sorry. Just enjoying the pizza."

"I'm glad." He took a long drink. "When were you thinking about starting?"

"As soon as possible. I've got a young, single mother. She's working full-time and taking classes in the evening, trying to get her degree. She's a perfect candidate. I'd love to get her into the house as soon as humanly possible."

He nodded. "Have I ever mentioned how much I admire what you do?"

She blushed. "It's nothing."

"You work full-time and spearhead HOMEs in your spare time, which from my perspective isn't all that spare. That's something. Something special, Callie."

Her cheeks got even redder. "So, what

movie did you bring?" she asked, blatantly changing the subject.

He let her. "I brought a chick flick just for you."

She visibly relaxed. "I think you secretly like them."

An hour into the film, she'd seemingly forgotten her discomfort completely.

An hour after that the film ended, and he let the credits play. Something in him melted as she sat and watched every name go by.

"That was nice," she said as after the James McDonalds' names had rolled by. "Thanks."

He stood. "It's getting late. I should go."

She didn't argue. "I'm glad you stopped by. Thanks for the movie, the pizza, and the help with the new project."

He gathered his folder and the movie rental and walked toward the door. Callie followed.

"I'll be in touch" was all he said. Then, before she could protest, he leaned down and kissed her the way he'd kissed her the first time. Only this time it was even sweeter, if that was possible.

Callie moved closer, her arms entwined around his neck. He wrapped his empty arm around her waist, encouraging her, deepening the kiss.

Suddenly she pulled back. "Noah, we have to talk about this. It's simply not appropriate, and I think —"

"Callie." He knew Callie was reluctant to take their relationship beyond a friendship. But he also suspected how very good they could have it.

He didn't want to listen to logic, didn't want to analyze and weigh the decision. He just wanted her. He wasn't sure how to make her understand that, and rather than risk saying the wrong thing and having her end things, he said, "I've got an early appointment tomorrow, so I really have to go. We'll talk about this later."

He grabbed his coat, opened the door, and made a beeline for his car.

"Noah Salo, you can't just kiss me and run."

He turned and laughed. "Ah, so you wish I'd kiss you and stay?"

"That's not what I'm saying."

"Callie, I think we'll have a better conversation later, when you've figured out just what you were saying. Gotta run. Night."

He got into the car and pulled out of her drive, grinning. One way or another, he was going to make Callie Smith see that they were meant to be together.

Chapter Eight

Callie knew an assault when she saw one. And this was an assault.

She'd barely poured her first cup of coffee when Julianna showed up on her doorstep.

"Callie, we need to talk" was her stepsister's preamble as she walked into the house and back to the kitchen and helped herself to a cup of coffee.

"About?" Callie asked.

"Noah called me. We talked about us . . . about you two."

Callie's morning cup of coffee turned to acid in her stomach. "There is no us two."

"But he'd like there to be."

"Listen." Callie picked up her mug to take another fortifying sip of coffee. "I'm not willing to risk our friendship on the off chance we could make a romance work."

"But, Callie —"

"Don't 'but, Callie' me. This is between Noah and me. Now, you can talk about anything with me . . . anything but this."

Julianna sighed heavily but obeyed and waxed enthusiastic about a new dress she'd found on sale. A dress she planned to wear on her next date with Darren Duffy.

Callie listened, sipping her coffee, despite being pretty sure it was eating a hole in her stomach. She knew that the fact that Julianna had moved from discussing sales to discussing dating Darren was a subtle bit of propaganda, designed to remind Callie her stepsister was moving beyond her failed relationship with Noah and that the course was clear for Callie to date him.

But Callie knew she didn't need to worry about dating Noah, since she planned on doing him in the next time she saw him. And, she realized, with the way he was acting, she probably wasn't going to have to wait too long.

She managed to shoo her sister out the door and went to the construction site. She spent her day taking her annoyance with Noah out on the nails she was hammering. After work, she went to her HOMEs house, still wearing her steel-toed boots, hoping Noah did show up so she could use them to kick some sense into him.

But it wasn't Noah who opened the door of the rundown house as she checked and rechecked her list of projects and materials. It was Dori.

"I heard I might find you here." She did a three-sixty. "This has potential."

"That's what I thought. A lot of cosmetics and a few major updates, and it will make a great home for someone." She looked around again herself, loving her mental picture of a family's making this house a home. "Just getting ready for the crews next week. I want to be sure I have everything they need on-site. You're working, aren't you?"

"I signed up for next week."

"Thanks."

"Don't thank me," Dori said. "Even if you weren't involved, HOMEs is a wonderful idea, and we're always happy to be part of a project."

"Thanks to your grandfather."

"You always try to do that, give the credit away. Papa's the first one to credit you with HOMEs' success. It's your baby. He just helped." Dori stopped and eyed Callie a moment.

That's when Callie knew. "He called you?"

"By *he,* you don't mean my grandfather but rather my brother, right?"

Callie nodded. She didn't really need Dori's answer.

"Maybe Noah did call and ask me to come out and encourage you to date him."

"What on earth is up with him? He's my friend. He's been my friend for years. Whatever it is he thinks has changed is just his way of reacting to breaking up with Julianna."

Dori didn't look convinced, but she didn't say anything.

"Dori, I mean it. Your brother and I are just friends."

"Noah says friendship is the best foundation for a relationship to be built on."

"Let me be clear about this," Callie said through clenched teeth. Slowly she enunciated each syllable. "It is not going to happen."

"Okay. Then that's that," Dori said, much too agreeably. "For the record, I don't blame you. I grew up with Noah. You just spent weekends and summers with us. I know all his little peccadillos."

"Peccadillos?"

"Foibles. Quirks," Dori supplied.

"I knew what *peccadillos* meant. I just don't hear the word bandied about very often."

"It's a good word." Dori was a word hound, frequently using obscure words she felt were too good to be ignored. "It deserves to be used. And Noah has plenty of peccadillos to talk about. Did you know you can't talk to him in the morning until he's had his coffee? If you try, you don't get a coherent response, just a grunt or two if you're lucky. And the mess. He's like a walking dump truck, leaving a trail of items behind him. Mom used to keep a basket in the front closet, and every day when she'd pick up the previous night's trail, she'd just dump them in and hand it to him. Oh, he was good-natured about putting it all away, but he didn't get the hint and just pick up after himself."

"I've experienced both, but come on, Dori, grumpy in the morning and a bit messy? That's the best you can do? Or, rather, the worst?"

"He's my brother. And despite his messiness and morning grumps, I think he's pretty wonderful and quite a catch. So I didn't come armed with a list of reasons not to date him. For the record, I think you should."

"That's some friend you are, Dori. I'll remember this when your day comes." Her voice full of as much foreboding as she could muster, she added, "If Nana Vancy has her way, your day is coming sooner than you think."

"Nice. Threaten the messenger. I can't help it if I think my brother's a catch and I'm friend enough to tell you that you'd be a fool to not give it a shot."

Callie couldn't think of an appropriate comeback, so she simply said, "I think we're done talking about Noah now."

"Suit yourself." Dori shrugged. "But if you change your mind, I made up a list of all his good qualities to balance out the grumpiness and messiness. Just give me a call, and I'll tell you all of them."

"I'm sure you did, and I'm sure you would, but don't hold your breath waiting for the call."

Dori was smiling, and it didn't dim at Callie's rather cranky-sounding words. "I'd better go now."

"Yeah, call your brother, and tell him his plan failed."

Why was he doing this? Pursuing her? She'd made her position clear. They were friends. They were both getting over relationships and didn't need to rebound with each other and possibly ruin a very good friendship.

She wasn't going to allow either of them to take that kind of chance.

Dori got to the door, turned, and said, "Oh, and, Callie?"

Callie looked up just as Dori said, "You will call and ask for the list."

Before Callie could retort, Dori was out the door. If her friend had waited, she'd have assured her that she wasn't going to call, but Dori was long gone.

Callie made an attempt to get back to her projects-and-materials lists, but she couldn't concentrate, so she went back to her Parade Street office and tried to work. When she still couldn't concentrate, she took to staring out the window at the steady stream of customers going into Nickel Plate Mills. The store had been on Parade Street as long as Callie could remember but had undergone some recent renovations. It was bigger and beautiful. A real asset to the revitalization of Parade Street.

Since she obviously wasn't going to get any work done, maybe she'd walk over and see what new things they had in stock at the store. Callie wasn't much of a shopper, but if she got the urge, a home-and-garden center was where she preferred to do her browsing.

She'd just turned off her computer when Nana Vancy came in.

Callie didn't groan, because she knew Nana would be offended. But she allowed herself a mental groan, along with a promise to herself that as soon as she got done listening to Nana Vancy's pitch, she was going to hunt Noah Salo down like the dog he was and tell him to back off.

"Nana, how nice to see you," she lied. "What brings you into HOMEs today? Did you want to volunteer on the new project? That last house Salo's worked on, you did the curtains. The new home owner loved them. They're still hanging. Maybe you'd consider helping me out on this one?"

"You know I will, *kedvenc,* but that's not why I'm here today. I'm here to tell you my grandson is a great catch. You should date him."

"Well, thanks, Nana. I'll take your opinion under advisement."

Nana snorted. "*Kedvenc,* you can't just placate the old lady and send her on her way." She pulled the visitor's chair around the desk and next to Callie's. "Tell me why you won't consider my grandson as a date."

"Did you forget he was supposed to marry my stepsister just a month ago?"

"They've both come to terms with that and agreed that they'd mistaken a deep friendship for something more than it was. They're friends. And I understand that Julianna herself came in to try to talk you into dating Noah, and that she's already dating someone else."

"Yes, Noah sicced Julianna on me. Along with Dori and now you. Don't you think it's rather cowardly of Noah to send others to fight his battles?"

"I think it's wise of him to realize he could use some help and call on us." She patted Callie's hand. "Now, you just tell Nana Vancy why you won't consider dating Noah. The real reason. You two are friends, and I know you used to have a crush on him."

"You're right. I did have a crush on him, but that was years ago. I was just a girl. A girl whose parents had divorced and found new spouses. I felt so alone, and Noah was so solid, and he came with a wonderful family. I think I had a crush on his family as much as on him."

"Oh, Callie, that's so sweet."

"It's the truth. But I'm all grown up now. Both my parents are happy, and I eventually realized that they didn't end my family, they just extended it."

"Oh, you should say those words to your mother and father. I'm sure they'd love to hear them. But just because your crush on Noah was years ago, that doesn't mean it's gone away. You're friends. You like the same sort of things. Why won't you at least see if that friendship can develop into something more?"

"Why?" Callie tried to find a way to explain why to someone else when she hardly understood it herself. "Why? Because . . . Because . . . Because of Mork and Moonlighting."

"Mork?" Nana looked confused.

Callie couldn't blame her. She'd felt nothing but confused since Noah kissed her. She knew she should just shut up with the crazy explanation, but she found that once the words started, there was no stopping their tumbling out. "On *Moonlighting,* when Maddie and David finally got together, the show started to fizzle. Same thing with *Mork and Mindy* and *X-Files* too, for that matter. And let's not even go into Mork and Mindy's supposed baby. That's a whole different discussion."

"I don't know *Mork and Mindy,*" Nana admitted.

Callie knew that her analogies were lost on Nana Vancy, so she tried to put her explanation into words that didn't require old-school television shows. "The thing those shows illustrated was that when friendships move from platonic to something more, things don't go well." She paused. "Oh, and Sam and Diane on

Cheers."

Nana shook her head. "Your whole generation watches too much television."

"You asked why, and that's why. It's anecdotal evidence that friendships should remain just that — friendships. Romance mucks things up."

"Your life isn't a TV show, *kedvenc.* Neither is Noah's. You're two people who deserve the best, and in this case, the best just might be each other."

"I'm sorry, Nana."

"I think you're being crazy with all your television reasons."

"I can't help how I feel."

"How you feel? I think that's what you should be asking yourself. How do you feel about Noah? If you think there's a chance you could love him, or that you do love him, you owe it to yourself and to him to give a more serious relationship a try."

"And if we try and things don't work out? I might lose his friendship," she said, voicing her very real fear. "I'm not willing to risk it."

"Julianna and Noah are still friends, and she broke their engagement just days before the wedding. If he could get over that, then I think that's just another foolish excuse."

Nana Vancy walked toward the door, then

turned around and said, "Think about it. And come see me if you need to talk."

She walked out and closed the door firmly behind her.

Callie decided that leaving her office was the wisest course. She didn't want to even guess who Noah was sending after her next. The best thing to do was not to be where they might find her.

That meant going home or back to the building site wasn't an option. And she was no longer in the mood to shop.

No, rather than hide, she was going to go beard the lion. She was going to track down Noah Salo and make him call off his helpers.

Then she planned to tell him that if he didn't stop this nonsense, their friendship was over.

Of course, ending their friendship was why she didn't want to date him in the first place. Okay, so her television analogies for Nana Vancy weren't really very valid. After all, Nana Vancy had been right — her life wasn't a televison show, so she didn't need to worry about ratings. She'd have to come up with a better argument for Noah.

When she got to his office, his secretary, Marilyn, grinned and said, "Callie, how nice to see you. Noah thought you might be stopping by —"

"I'm sure he did," Callie muttered, more to herself than to Marilyn.

"— and that if you did, I should tell you he went home and is waiting for you there."

"Thanks. I'll track him down." She started toward the door. Oh, yeah, she was going to track him down all right. Then she was going to read him the riot act and make him stop this nonsense.

"Oh, Callie," Marilyn called, stopping her in her tracks. "Noah also told me that I should feel free to wax poetic about what a great guy he is."

"He told you to wax poetic?"

Marilyn laughed. "Okay, you caught me. Those weren't his exact words. I think it went something more like, 'Tell Callie I'm great, okay? Tell her to date me.' But 'wax poetic' sounds better." She picked up a sheet of paper from her desk. "Rather than hold you up, I wrote down a list of great Noah qualities. I especially like number five."

Callie glanced down at the list. "Number five. Knows when to listen?" She tried not to laugh out loud at that one. If Noah Salo knew how to listen, he'd have heard her say that she wasn't interested in anything more than a friendship with him.

She looked back up at Marilyn, ready to give her back her list, but something in the woman's expression stopped her.

"You don't know what an important quality listening is. You see, last year, when I had a number of family things hit all at once, Noah brought me coffee every morning and asked, 'How're things today?' It wasn't just a social question. I know because the first time he asked, I said something about everything's being all right. He gave me *the look.* The one I've seen his grandmother use on his grandfather. Then he repeated the question as he sat down in the chair across from me and really listened while I told him. He helped me through everything, and he's just my boss. I figure that bodes well for any woman he's involved with."

Callie wasn't sure what to say to that. She didn't know if she should apologize, thank Marilyn, or simply tell her that she should mind her own business. That not everyone wanted to spill their guts to strangers. She counted to ten and simply tucked the list into her pocket and went with, "Thanks."

"Another thing. He's still friends with Julianna, after how she dumped him and everything." Marilyn caught herself. "Sorry. She's your stepsister, isn't she?"

"No problem. The fact that he is friends with her says something." Callie knew that it was a huge hole in her I-can't-date-him-and-risk-ruining-our-friendship argument. He'd obviously proven he could maintain a friendship after a relationship ended. "I'd better go now."

The ride out to his Greene Township home seemed to take longer than she remembered its being. Her mind went in circles, one thought chasing the other as she tried to sort out what to do about Noah Salo and his very strange campaign.

She was always surprised at how much more snow Greene Township had than Erie proper. It was only a ten- or fifteen-minute drive away. But as cold air passed over the lake, it hit a ridge of land that I-90 followed and dumped all the moisture it had absorbed over the lake onto Greene Township. She was glad she was driving her four-wheel-drive truck.

She got to Noah's and was relieved that his hilly driveway was plowed. Even with four-wheel drive, she wouldn't have tried it if it wasn't. She parked, trudged through the snow to the front door, and knocked.

"Callie," Noah said, his pleasure at seeing her evident. "Come on in out of the cold."

"I'm not feeling overly cold right now,

Noah. As a matter of fact, I'm feeling rather hot under the collar."

"May I take your coat?"

She watched as he hung up the coat, then turned back to her and smiled. He was wearing a worn pair of jeans and a very soft flannel shirt. His hair was slightly mussed. And as she looked at him, she realized that he was beautiful.

She smiled at the thought, sure that Noah wouldn't be impressed by the description.

"I was just thinking about you when you knocked on the door," he said conversationally as he led her into the living room.

"Were you?"

He nodded as he sat on the couch and patted the cushion next to him.

She wanted to go sit in a chair and keep as much distance as possible between them, but she thought it might appear rather churlish, so she sat on the couch, but as close to the edge as possible.

"You've been on my mind a lot today too," she said sweetly.

He looked pleased. "Oh? Do tell."

"Of course you've been. After all, my sister, your grandmother, and even your secretary —"

"Marilyn's my personal assistant," he corrected.

"Personal assistant," she parroted. "You even conned her into joining . . ." She searched for the right word and finally settled on, ". . . your campaign."

"You don't look happy about it."

"You thought I would be? You thought I'd be impressed to have you chase me like this? You're supposed to be my friend, so I'd have thought you'd know better. What were you thinking?" Before he could answer, she continued, "Noah, I don't know what game you're playing, but I don't want to be a part of it."

"Listen, I want us to date, and I thought having a few people giving me testimonials couldn't hurt."

"You've never needed testimonials," she told him softly. "At least not with me. I know what a wonderful guy you are. You're a good friend. But —"

"But. There's that but. Give me a good reason. I mean, tell me you don't think you'll ever think of me that way. I'll probably call you a liar. When we've kissed, you haven't been unmoved."

"No, you're right, I can't say I couldn't feel that way about you. But I will say, I don't want to."

"Why? You still haven't given me a good reason. And when Nana called, she said you had some excuses she didn't understand about Orks and bars. I'm not sure what that was, but I doubt it will impress me any more than it impressed her."

"It was *Mork and Mindy* and *Cheers.* My point to your grandmother was that friendships don't translate into romances well. And we are friends. I don't want to lose that." Even to herself, it sounded lame.

"You forgot *Moonlighting.* When friends become more, something . . . what was the word? *Fizzles?*"

"You're mocking me."

"I'm not. I don't think that's the real reason. I'm not sure what's standing in the way. I wish you'd explain it to me. Because maybe we wouldn't fizzle. Maybe we'd ignite. Maybe we'd be like be like Daphne and Niles."

"Huh?" she asked.

"With all your television references, I'd have thought you'd get that one right off. Didn't you watch *Frasier?*"

"Yes," she admitted. And as she remembered Niles and Daphne, she realized what he was going to say.

"Then you'll remember that Frasier's brother and his housekeeper had a romance that did work. There was something between them for several seasons, and when they finally got together, he was still head-over-heels for her. I'm pretty sure I'd still be head-over-heels for you."

"What do you mean, *still?*" She regretted asking the question the minute the words were out of her mouth.

Noah sort of smiled as he got up and walked around his desk.

She wasn't sure where to go, what to do.

"Let me show you what I mean by *still.*"

"Cut it out, Noah. Stop making those googly-eyes at me."

"Googly-eyes?" He laughed, shaking his head. "Callie, I'm crazy about you."

"Since when? We're friends. We've always been friends. I was the tagalong. The side-kick. Your fishing buddy. You never once looked at me as anything more."

"I'm looking now."

"There they are again, those googly-eyes. Just stop it."

"Callie."

"Coming here was a mistake. I'm going."

"Callie, come on."

She shook her head. "Listen, Noah, we are friends, and that hasn't changed, but I think we need some space while you get over whatever this is."

"I don't think it's going to be that easy to get over."

"Call me when you've managed it."

Noah realized he'd made a tactical error. He crossed off all the other friends and family members he'd planned to enlist in his get-Callie-to-date-me campaign. He needed a new plan.

She wouldn't date him because of *Mork and Mindy*?

He smiled.

He knew just what he needed to do, and he headed to the computer for a little online shopping.

Two days later, the doorbell rang just as Callie was about to pop a microwave dinner in. She opened the door to find a box from an online bookstore. It was heavier than a paperback, and she couldn't remember ordering anything, although she did a lot of her shopping online because it was so much easier than wandering around the mall looking for an item. Just get online, make a couple clicks, and some nice delivery person brought it within the week.

The last thing she'd ordered was her outfit for Julianna and Noah's stag party. Thinking about her sister and Noah was the last thing Callie wanted to do, so she concentrated on the package instead. Curiosity won out over her slight case of Noah-withdrawal. She hadn't heard a peep from him since she'd left his house the other night. And that was good. She wasn't interested in hearing from him, at least not until he'd come to his senses.

She took the box into the living room, rummaged through the end table drawer for a pair of scissors, and cut through the packing tape.

She opened the box and found a complete series pack of *Frasier* DVDs. She wanted to be annoyed at Noah's newest onslaught, but instead she laughed.

She sat on her couch, laughing like crazy. It was a good ploy — the kind that begged to be shared with someone. On the heels of that thought, she realized that the person she'd most like to share it with was . . . Noah.

She thought about how often in the past, he'd been one of the first people she'd gone to with news or questions.

Even after her breakup with Jerry, she hadn't gone to her stepsister or friends. She'd gone to Noah. She'd known she could count on him to comfort her. Just as she'd known that she'd feel better after he did.

Maybe he was right.

Maybe there was something between them

— something more than just a good friendship.

Marilyn's list of Noah's qualities was still in her room. Maybe she should read it.

She'd tucked it away two days ago when she got home. She hadn't planned on reading it. After all, she didn't need any help seeing Noah's good qualities. She knew them all.

She'd ignored it all that night and the next. Ignored it as she ate meals. Ignored it at work and at HOMEs. She'd even ignored it as she took a bubble bath tonight.

Now she was going to be forced to ignore nine complete seasons of *Frasier* as well?

Well, she could manage it. She'd just watch something on televison. She flipped aimlessly through the channels, and she found a repeat of *Frasier* on. It was if the entire cosmos was conspiring against her.

And she decided to give up the battle. She opened season one. She fell asleep three episodes into the series and dreamed of Niles and Daphne double-dating with her and Noah.

Which was why she was up at 1:36 in the morning. She turned off the TV and DVD player and stumbled into the bedroom and into pajamas.

But sleep eluded her.

She finally got up and took Marilyn's list of Noah's good qualities out of her vanity drawer.

~ Punctual.
~ Fairly neat.
~ Kind.
~ Smells good. (Callie, I don't want you to think I go around sniffing Noah, but I'm sure you've noticed he always smells nice. That's a plus.)
~ Knows how to listen.
~ Loyal. (Not like a dog is loyal to his owner, but rather like a guy who would never cheat on you.)
~ Someone you can depend on.

Not one of them came as a surprise.

What was she going to do about Noah Salo?

He wasn't giving up.

An idea slowly formed in her sleepiness-fogged mind. Maybe she should help him along.

Disregarding that it was now after two in the morning, she dialed Noah's number.

"Hello?" he answered after a number of rings.

"Fine. You win. I'll go out on one date. But if it goes horribly, you have to give up and admit we're just friends."

"And if it goes as well as I expect it will go?"

"Then I'll agree to another date."

"Five other dates."

"Fine," she agreed, knowing that their date would be anything but a success. "Call me tomorrow, and we'll work out the details." She started to hang up but heard him call her name.

"Callie, are you still there?"

"Yes."

"I just wanted to say, thanks for giving me a try."

"It's not you I'm worried about. It's me. But we're not going to talk about it tonight. Call me tomorrow. Good night."

And before he could say anything else, she hung up.

Noah Salo had no idea what he was in for.

CHAPTER NINE

Friday night.

Date night.

Callie had planned on making it her new gym night. She figured if she wasn't dating anyone, she might as well get her workout in Friday night so she could sleep in guilt-free on Saturday morning.

She wished she was at the gym as she stood outside Waves, a restaurant down on Erie's dock. It was far fancier than she normally enjoyed. As were her clothes. She'd worn a dress Julianna had made her buy last season. Her stepsister had insisted that a knee-length black dress was timeless and a good investment, but this was only the second time in almost a year that Callie had found a reason to wear it. And she wasn't enjoying the experience.

Taking a deep breath, she went into the restaurant.

Noah had wanted to pick her up, but

she'd insisted on meeting him. He hadn't argued.

She walked up to the maître d'. "I'm meeting a . . ." She hesitated, not wanting to use the word *date,* even though that's exactly what she'd agreed to. Since Noah wasn't around, she went ahead and substituted the word ". . . *friend.*"

"Ah, the gentleman arrived early. I'll show you back."

The maître d' led her through a maze of tables to the back of the restaurant. There, in the most remote corner of the ultra-swanky room, sat Noah. He was wearing dark pants and a crisp white shirt, and he looked good. Very good.

He stood as she approached. "You came," he said as he pulled her chair out for her.

"I told you I would."

The maître d' obviously sensed he wasn't needed and said, "I'll send your waiter back," as he left.

"I wasn't sure you would come," Noah admitted as he took his own seat. "Here's a menu." He handed her a fancy, leather-bound menu.

What Callie was dying for was a good hamburger and maybe a strawberry milkshake, neither of which was evident on the menu.

She didn't know what to order here. And to be honest, she wasn't sure she'd even taste anything she did order. Her stomach was in knots, and her palms were sweaty. What on earth was wrong with her? She's shared countless meals with Noah. They were friends, first and foremost. She had to forget this was a date.

"I'm glad you finally agreed to the date," Noah said, as if on cue.

"I'm trying to forget it's a date, thank you very much."

He gave her a long look. "You're really freaked out."

"Yes."

"I don't get it, Callie. We've been friends for so long. Why is it so hard for you to consider moving beyond our friendship to something more?"

"Noah, I don't want to lose your friendship if it doesn't work out."

"We've been through this. The fact that Julianna and I are still friends shows that wouldn't have to be the case."

"I . . ." She sighed. "Listen, here's the long and the short of it. I don't believe in love. At least, not in the same way you and your whole family seem to. Not that one-true-love, happily-ever-after sort of thing, anyway."

"Callie —" he started to protest, but she cut him off.

"Noah, when I was growing up, my parents seemed happy, until one day they came in and told me they were getting a divorce. My mom remarried and seems happy, and you've seen my dad and Julianna's mom together. They're blissful. Then there's your sister, Vancy, and Matt. And let's not forget you and Julianna."

"Hey," he protested.

"No, seriously. The two of you loved each other enough to think you should get married, and now here you are, wanting to date me, and there she is, dating Darren. You've both recovered from your almost-wedding. It sort of proves my point. Love doesn't last."

"It can, when it's right."

"But how on earth can you tell if it's right? Maybe when you're celebrating a fiftieth anniversary you can look back and say, yes, we were the real deal. But most people who fall in love think it's real . . . until it isn't."

"I don't believe that," he insisted.

"But I do. And that, if for no other reason, is why we'd never make it."

"Callie."

She braced herself for his next argument, but all he said was, "Fine. If that's how you feel, that's how you feel. Let's just forget I mentioned the dating business and have a nice meal."

"You mean it?"

"Yes. You are, first and foremost, my friend." He picked up his menu. "So, what looks good to you?"

Callie picked up her own menu and studied it, trying to ignore the little niggle of annoyance that was eating away at her. Here she was, pouring her soul out to Noah, telling him things she'd never shared with anyone, things she hardly even dared think about herself, and he just said, *fine, let's eat?*

No trying to convince her she was wrong?

No list of reasons love could work?

Just, *let's eat?*

She studied the menu, determined not to let Noah Salo see how confused he'd made her.

Callie kept shooting Noah puzzled looks. There was a mixture of annoyance in the looks as well.

He pretended not to notice as he purposefully kept the conversation light. He talked about work. He talked about HOMEs. He watched as Callie visibly relaxed.

He tried to decide what to do now. How could he reach her, make her see that they should be together?

She had a valid point. He'd been engaged, but in hindsight, he realized he and Julianna had confused friendship with love.

He'd done the same thing with Callie, in reverse.

He'd thought of her as a friend and come to realize she was more than that.

He loved her.

It might seem fast, but he knew it was anything but. This was a love that had grown quietly for years. One built firmly on friendship.

He built homes for a living, and he knew that the quality of a structure depended upon its foundation. He and Callie had the best foundation possible.

Now he needed to convince her of that.

He'd tried enlisting other people's help. That hadn't worked.

He'd tried wooing her into dating him with no greater success. She'd been a nervous wreck until he'd told her the evening didn't constitute a date. That's when she'd visibly relaxed.

He'd lied. He did consider the evening a date. And in his mind, the date was going well. And she'd agreed that if it went well, she'd be open to others.

He tried to hide his smile as his new

course of action laid itself out in his mind.

He wasn't going to woo her, wasn't going to ask other people to help. He was just going to date Callie . . . and not mention it. He'd ask her out, and if she assumed it was merely one friend asking another, not a boyfriend asking a girlfriend, that wasn't his fault.

She'd relaxed the moment she'd decided they were not really on a date. So, he'd just let her go on thinking that, and later he'd explain, after she'd grown accustomed to dating him.

Okay, it wasn't much of a plan, but it was all he had.

"Dessert?" he asked as they finished their meal.

Callie smiled. "Sure. Why not?"

He walked her to her car that night and then went home to plan.

The next day he showed up at the Salo construction site at lunch, two bags of Mc-Donalds in hand along with some preliminary plans for the HOMEs house.

He left, pleased that they'd had a lunch date.

The next day, he met her at the HOMEs house after work and brought her a candy bar.

His new dating-but-not-telling-Callie plan

176

was brilliant. He'd managed a lunch date and had taken her the traditional chocolates, and she was none the wiser.

Noah wasn't sure how long he could manage to date Callie without her knowing, but he hoped that by the time she realized how things stood, she'd have gotten over her fears and realized what he already knew — they were meant to be together.

The next few weeks were some of the nicest in Callie's life. Noah had stopped his campaign to date her. Instead, he'd gone back to being a good friend. More than a good friend. They spent more and more time together. It began to feel natural to talk to him at lunch and plan their evening together. Dinner at her house, or his, or even out.

Winter was losing its grip on the region, and as the weather warmed, work picked up, and though both of them got busier, the habits they'd started to build held firm.

Callie spent a weekend at the new HOMEs house, cutting down a tree that had fallen during one of the winter's worst storms. The melting snow had turned the backyard into a swamp, but just being out in forty-degree temperatures felt almost balmy.

Noah was there helping. It seemed that every time she turned around, Noah was there. But since he'd stopped all his dating talk, it didn't bother her at all. Things felt comfortable again, as if they'd gotten back to their normal footing.

Her arms were ready to give out, so she turned off the chain saw and set it down for a minute.

Noah saw her and followed suit. He took off his ear protection and grinned at her. "It was bigger than it looked."

"That's one of the reasons I loved this house. It has old trees and a feeling of permanence. It's really coming together. I'm just so grateful to be outside working again. The house was a lot of interior work, which made it a perfect winter project, but I'm glad it's drawing to an end."

"The winter or the project?"

"Both." She looked at him, covered in sawdust and wearing torn jeans and a faded denim jacket, and realized she liked this look much more than she liked his business-suit look. Although he did look nice in a suit as well.

To be honest, Noah looked nice in whatever he wore.

And thinking about Noah's looking nice made her nervous. That's not how friends and buddies thought about each other.

She thrust her ear protection back onto her head, picked up the saw, and pulled the starter.

She wasn't going to think about him like that anymore.

A week later, Noah pulled up in front of the HOMEs house, pleased to see daffodils and hyacinths sprouting in the front yard.

He enjoyed working with Callie on the HOMEs construction site. He'd long since encouraged his crew not to come. It gave him a great excuse to be alone with Callie. Because he realized that working on a house wasn't the best date, he made sure to do something date-ish each night.

Tonight he'd brought flowers.

Granted, they were salvias for around the house, but they were flowers, and he was giving them to Callie, which meant the date she didn't realize was a date was official.

He grabbed the pallet from the back of the truck and carried it to the house.

Callie opened the door, wearing paint-splattered clothes. "What do you have there?"

"I brought you flowers." He held them out to her, looking very pleased with himself.

Callie took the tray of plants and sniffed.

"Oh, Noah, they're prettier than they smell. I'm sure they'll look wonderful around the house."

"They're perennials, so there won't be much upkeep to them."

"I just finished painting the living room, which means, once these are planted, we're done."

"Which makes the bottle of wine and pizza in the cab of the truck not just dinner but a celebration. Why don't we plant the flowers first? The pizza will keep a bit."

"Perfect."

They made short order of planting the flowers. He spread a tarp from the back of his truck on the empty living room floor, placed the pizza in the center, and pulled the wineglasses and paper towels he'd brought out of the bag, then poured the wine.

"To us," he said, handing Callie a glass and toasting.

She quirked an eyebrow and corrected him. "To the house."

"To the house," he agreed. As the glass reached her lips, he added, "And to us. We make a great couple."

Her eyes narrowed as she finished the sip. "Noah, it's been weeks. I thought you'd let the couple thing die."

"I never said that."

"But you haven't mentioned it."

He grinned in a way that made her decidedly nervous. "Noah, what are you up to?"

He sipped his wine and shot her his well-practiced innocent look. "What do you think I'm up to?"

"I think you're up to no good."

"I'm hurt, Callie." He upped the wattage of his innocent look to such a degree that Callie fully expected a shiny halo to appear above his head and harps to start playing in the background.

"I know that look, Noah Salo. You used it on your mother that time she wanted to know who ate the cake. You gave her that look and said, 'Who do you think ate the cake?' You countered her question by parroting it back, to avoid lying."

"Callie, I'm really not sure what you think is going on here, but the pizza in my hand and the wine in my glass seem to indicate dinner."

"Yes. Dinner. That's all it is. We're working together and eating together. That's all."

"Callie, that's not all. We've been dating since that dinner at Waves six weeks ago."

"What?" Callie glanced at her glass and wondered if she'd had more wine than she thought she'd had. "What did you say?"

Slowly, enunciating each word, Noah repeated, "You said, if that first date went well, we could continue dating, and it did, so we have. We've been secretly dating for the last six weeks."

"Pardon?" She set her wineglass down with a thud. "I must have misheard you. It sounded like you said we've been dating."

"Secretly dating," he clarified.

"Noah, what you're saying is that our dating was such a secret that *I* didn't even know about it?"

He nodded, looking very pleased with himself. "Yeah, that made it kind of cool, don't you think?"

"You're crazy." She needed to get out of here. She stood as she assured him, "You can't date someone without their knowing it."

He stood as well. "Sure you can. We've done the whole dating gamut. Lunches, dinners. I've brought you chocolates —" She must have looked as confused as she felt, because he clarified. "Chocolate bars, but they still count as the traditional, date-a-girl-bring-her-chocolates sort of thing."

He had brought her a number of chocolate bars of late, but she hadn't thought anything of it.

"Look at tonight," he continued, nodding

at their impromptu picnic. "Dinner. Flowers. That's a date."

"It's pizza, which we've shared countless times in the past, and you never counted it as a dinner date. And the flowers were for the house, not me, so they don't count either."

"No, the flowers were for you. All the meals, all the chocolates, all the flowers. It's all been for you, about you, because I'm dating you."

"Stop saying that." She leaned over and started to clear up the picnic, wishing she could clear up Noah's misconceptions as easily. "We're not dating."

"Listen, I wish I could have told you sooner, but you seemed so uncomfortable with the idea. I thought it best to sort of ease you into it. But we're dating — that's the truth of the matter."

"We're not dating." She felt as if she was repeating herself, but she couldn't think of anything else. They weren't dating. "We're not."

"You can say it, but it doesn't alter the fact that we've been dating for weeks. And I must say, it's going swimmingly well."

"And you can't make it so by simply saying so," she told him as she put the last paper plate into the garbage bag and sealed it up. She started unplugging all her power tools. She had to get out of there before Noah told her they were engaged and she didn't know it, or even worse, that they'd gotten married without her being aware of it.

"Noah, you're crazy." She'd said it before, but it needed to be said again. "Really, crazy."

"About you." He grinned.

"Oh, that's so bad." She laughed despite herself. "Really bad."

He was obviously unrepentant. "So, we're going to have to seal the deal."

"Huh?"

"Listen, we've been dating for weeks, and I haven't pushed the issue, but it's time for a kiss, don't you think? I mean, I brought you dinner, wine, and flowers. Now, you kiss me and say, *Thank you, Noah.*"

"I'm going to say, *Noah, you need professional help.*" She knew she wasn't going to beat him at whatever he was up to, so she decided to stop playing. "I need to go."

"And I need help, all right. From you."

"I'm not kissing you," she said with all the firmness she could muster. And mustering firmness was hard because, as she looked at him, grinning like a loon, telling her that they'd been dating though she didn't know it, she realized that he was crazy . . . and she was crazy about him.

She wanted to kiss him, though she didn't want to want to.

Her weird turns of logic were making her dizzy. "It's time to call it a night, Noah."

"Ah, you'd rather kiss me good night than kiss me for dinner. I can't say I blame you. I don't want you to think I'm trying to bribe you into that kiss. I want you to want to."

"But I don't want to," she assured him.

He just looked at her, giving her that stare his grandmother had taught him. It was the one that said you're-lying-and-that-hurts-you-more-than-it-hurts-me.

"Fine, I don't want to want to."

"But you do?" he asked triumphantly.

She nodded.

"So, if you want to, and I want to, what's stopping us?"

"Common sense is stopping us. We're not dating."

"Callie."

She tried to think of an argument. Something articulate that would make her position clear to him. But Callie couldn't come up with anything, so she settled for saying, "Argh."

"Argh?" He laughed. "That's the best argument you've got? 'Argh'?"

" 'Argh' is the perfect argument. It's the best word to use when no other word will do."

"Listen, Callie, most dates end in a kiss. I've been patient, but it's been weeks."

She tried once again to clarify things. "Noah, you can't date someone who doesn't know she's dating you."

"You can, and I did." He smiled and continued. "We have been dating. We've been together almost every night since our honeymoon, as a matter of fact."

"It wasn't *our* honeymoon. It was *your* honeymoon."

"Listen, I know we've done things in an unorthodox way. We were friends who went on a honeymoon before we started dating."

"You were dating. I wasn't dating."

"You were. You just didn't know it. And now that you do, you're nervous."

"Huh?"

" 'Argh' now, huh?" He tsked. "Callie, we're going to have to work on expanding your vocabulary."

"I've got to go."

"Chicken."

"Huh?" Noah quirked an eyebrow, and Callie tried for a more articulate, "What did you say?"

"You're afraid. For all your talk about

186

Mork and Mindy, your parents, and Julianna and me — the truth is, you're afraid I'll hurt you. That I'll walk away. But, Callie, I'm not walking anywhere but toward you. Maybe, early on, I could have gone in another direction, but now? I couldn't if I wanted to. And I don't want to."

"Noah, this is ridiculous. I'm not afraid."

"Once upon a time, I'd have believed that. You were the most fearless girl I ever met. You threw yourself into life with abandon. What happened?"

"I grew up. But I'm cautious now, not afraid."

"Prove it. Kiss me."

"Noah —"

"Kiss me, Callie. If you're as immune to me as you think, it won't be difficult. But if I'm right, if there's more to your feelings than you're letting on, then . . ." He shrugged and grinned.

"You're awfully sure of yourself," she muttered.

"No, I'm awfully sure of you. You like me."

"I never denied that —"

"Really like me. As a matter of fact, you're falling in love with me."

"How on earth do you get through doorways with a head that swollen?" She was exasperated. She didn't know how to argue

Noah's points.

"You're trying to change the subject. Kiss me, Callie."

"You promise, if I kiss you and I don't swoon, you'll stop this?"

"You'll swoon."

She shook her head and walked over to him and planted a chaste kiss on his cheek. "There. You've been kissed, and I felt nothing."

"That wasn't a kiss."

"My lips were on —"

"My cheek. It doesn't count."

She sighed and kissed his lips this time, in the same brusque, platonic way.

"Ba-bawk, ba-bawk." Noah whispered his best chicken impression.

"Cut that out."

"Then kiss me like you mean it. Show me you're not afraid."

Callie knew she didn't have to prove anything to anyone, but the idea of kissing Noah was tempting. Too tempting to resist.

She approached slowly and kissed him. Like she meant it. She wasn't sure how long the kiss lasted, but she knew that somewhere along the line, she'd forgotten to breathe. When she broke off the kiss, she spent a moment trying to remember how to.

Noah didn't say anything. He just stood

there grinning.

"I told you I wasn't afraid."

"You're right. You weren't. But you did feel something."

She'd forgotten that she was supposed to be proving she didn't care.

"Go ahead and say it. We're Niles and Daphne, not Mork and Mindy."

"No."

"You'll say it eventually. I'll wait."

He started gathering up the remains of their picnic. "So, tomorrow Nana Vancy's having a little to-do at the house. I thought we'd go, if you're agreeable."

"Noah, we're not dating, so you don't have to clear your plans with me. Go to your grandmother's. Have a good time."

"That kiss just proved we are dating — have been for weeks. And I do have to check, because I want to spend my time with you. If you don't want to go to Nana's, we'll find something else to do."

"Argh," she said again, but when he gave her that triumphant look, she added, "You're infuriating."

"Yes, I am. Wanna kiss me again?"

"If I say yes and go with you to Nana Vancy's, that's not proving anything, okay?"

He grinned. "See? I knew you couldn't resist me."

"You're nuts."

"About you. Just admit it — we're a couple."

"No."

"Then tell me why you're afraid."

"Noah, you were set to marry someone else just a few months ago."

"I was confused."

"My stepsister."

"She was confused too. We've worked it out. We're friends. I don't see that it's an obstacle."

"We're friends too. That's an obstacle."

"We've gone over all this. Tell me what's really going on."

"I don't believe in love the way you do."

He scoffed.

"Seriously." She wanted him to understand. "I tried to explain it before. I know how transient love can be. My parents seemed to be happy, but they divorced and moved on to new spouses. You were set to marry Julianna. You two broke up, and now she's happy with Darren."

"And I'm happy as well — with you."

"Noah —"

"And you've just proved my case. Your parents loved each other, but it wasn't that lifetime love. They've both found that now. That's something to celebrate. And I never denied that I loved Julianna. But it wasn't the real deal for me or for her. That's why we've both been able to move on, to find the real thing. That's why she's happy with Darren, and I'm happy with you."

"You're not with me."

"I'm in love with you, Callie. And it's real."

He could sense she wasn't ready for more, so he simply said, "I'll pick you up after work, and we'll go to Nana's together. And I promise — Scout's honor — that I won't mention our dating or being in love. I won't even kiss you."

"Thank you."

"But you're welcome to kiss me."

"It's time to go. I'll see you tomorrow."

"And you'll dream about me tonight. About what we could have."

"Nightmares, Noah. They'll be nightmares."

He just laughed. He could sense she was weakening. Somehow he was going to figure out how to convince Callie Smith that she was his one and only, just as he was hers.

CHAPTER TEN

The next night, Noah showed up at Callie's house, a bouquet of daisies in hand. "Now that we're not secretly dating, I can bring you flowers out in the open. I thought about roses, but that's not your flower. I wandered around the shop forever, trying to decide what yours was, and then it hit me. Daisies."

"I'm a weed?" she asked.

"No Daisies grow wild and independently. They grow wherever they like, in gardens and fields. They're tough and beautiful." He leaned down and, before she could say anything, kissed her cheek. "Like you," he finished.

Callie was so flustered, she didn't say much on the short drive from her house to the Salos'.

For as long as she'd been coming to stay with her father's new family, Callie had loved being part of any Salo celebration. Here was a family that stayed together through thick and thin. A family who saw their children not just on holidays and summer vacations. Here was the family she'd always dreamed of having.

Perfect.

Walking in with Noah, she felt like a fraud. He was playing at being her boyfriend.

Maybe it was the thrill of the chase. After losing Julianna, he had to prove to himself he was still in the game.

Even as she had the thought, she discarded it. Noah didn't need to prove anything to anyone, not even himself. And he didn't play games.

He draped his arm casually over her shoulders. "Hey, Nana, look who I brought with me."

"Callie, *kedvenc.* You come in, and let me get you a chair. Ricky, you're a gentleman. Get up and give the lady your chair."

"I'm no gen'leman. I'm a boy."

"And boys have to get up for ladies too, or else they don't get any of Nana's banana pudding."

Rick jumped out of his chair with the vigor of someone who'd sat on a pin. His twin brother, Chris, jumped out of his as well. "If you take our seats, you gotta read us a story," he said with a grin that reminded Callie of Noah.

"I think that's a very fair trade. Why don't you two go pick one out?"

The twins raced out of the room and were back in an instant with *The Wild Baby Book*. "Again?" Callie asked, laughing. She'd read this particular book frequently in the past.

"Yep," Chris said.

"I'll sit in Callie's lap," Rick told Chris, " 'cause she's in my chair, so it's only fair. You sit next to us." To Callie he added, "We're almost too big for laps but not yet, Aunt Vancy says."

"Okay," Chris agreed. "But maybe you can tell us another story after, and I can have your lap?" he asked as he climbed into the chair.

"That sounds fair to me," Callie agreed. "*The Wild Baby Book* by Barbro Lindgren, translated by Jack Prelutsky," she started.

"*Translated* means it was in a different language first," Ricky told her, parroting what she'd told him the last time.

"You're right," she assured him, and she read the book about a very bad little boy whose antics made the twins laugh time after time.

"That was a good one," Chris said, as if it was the first time he'd ever heard the story. "Do you want the other one now?"

"What about after dinner?" she countered.

"Okay. Come on, Rick, let's go dig for worms. Maybe Grandpa Bela will take us fishin' tomorrow."

Without another word, the boys left. Callie looked up and found Noah in the archway between the living room and dining room, holding two glasses and watching her.

"What?" she asked.

"You're good with kids." He came and took the seat Chris had vacated, and Callie wished she'd suggested they read the second book now rather than later.

"So," Noah continued conversationally, handing her a glass.

Callie took a long sip of the lemonade.

"How many do you think we should have?" he asked.

Callie choked on the drink. "What?"

"How many kids should we have?" he repeated. "My sister's got the two boys and another on the way. And of course, my parents had three kids. It's a nice number. But I don't want to think of this as a race, that we have to keep up with any of them."

"You promised you wouldn't talk about —"

"Being in love with you. And I'm not. I'm just talking about our future children."

She laughed, which wasn't her intent. She'd intended to be annoyed. But she couldn't manage it. Because . . .

Because she loved Noah.

It should have been some totally unexpected realization, but this was no lightbulb-over-the-head moment. Maybe that's because she'd always loved him, even when she wasn't ready to admit it, even to herself.

She looked at him, grinning from ear to ear at his newest weird logic. He'd kept his promise and not mentioned love, but in mentioning their future children, he'd reminded her of everything that was going on.

"So, how many kids?" he pressed.

Callie realized that the thought of having Noah's baby didn't annoy her. As a matter of fact, the image of that imaginary baby melted her.

She'd dated a lot of men over the years, but none of them had worked out, and that hadn't come as a shock. She'd known from the beginning of every relationship that it wouldn't last. She'd dated some of the men because they'd been nice, or fun, or great conversationalists. She'd liked all of them, but she'd never loved them. Had known from their first dates that she'd couldn't love them.

But Noah?

She loved him.

She'd lied when she said she didn't believe in the real thing. Lied to him. Lied to herself. Because looking at Noah, Callie realized that she did believe.

More than that, she realized they were, in fact, Niles and Daphne.

"Callie? I'm not sure what that look means, but you're making me nervous."

"You were talking about babies. Call me traditional, but that means marriage, right?"

"Huh?"

She tsked. "Really, Noah, you need to work on your vocabulary."

"Marriage? That wasn't a word I expected to hear from you."

"Well, we've been engaged for weeks. Talking about marriage is only natural."

"Engaged?"

She grinned. "Sure. If you can date me without my knowing, I guess I can be engaged to you without your knowing. So it's not sudden. Marry me."

Noah took her into his arms and kissed her. And though they'd kissed before, it was like the first time for Callie, because now, finally, she was admitting what she had to have always known. Noah was the one.

The only one for her.

The real thing.

"You know," he said, when he finally

released her, "the media will love this story."

"Then let's elope." She hadn't known she was going to say the words until she heard herself say them. "I don't want this to be about your grandmother's curse. I don't want it to be a media circus. I want it to be about you and me, about our being Niles and Daphne."

"You mean it, don't you?" he asked, disbelief in his voice.

Callie nodded. "I love you, Noah. I think I've known it for a long time. You're right — I was simply afraid to admit it."

"My grandmother —"

"Will be thrilled you're happily married. And, Noah, you will be happy. I mean, I'm still not going to be girly. I don't cook much, and I'll never have a great manicure, but I love you."

"Let's go."

"You mean it?" She hugged him and realized how right he felt in her embrace.

"Yes. Do you?"

She nodded.

"What changed?"

"When you asked me about having a baby, I realized, I'd love to have your baby. And there's something else. I realized that I may have dated before, but I'd known from the first that none of them was going to last.

When I caught Jerry cheating, the third bad break in a row, I wondered why. Now, I realize, I dated losers on purpose. I set myself up in relationships that were bound to fail because — you were right — I was afraid."

"And now?"

"I'm not afraid anymore — at least, not with you." She said the words with absolute certainty. With Noah, she would never be afraid.

He pulled her into his arms and kissed her, and she kissed him back. It was a promise on her part, a vow, as serious as any marriage vow. She was saying, *I love you, and that won't change.*

"We'd better get out of here before Nana catches wind of this, or she'll be calling the papers herself," Noah said, tugging her out of the room.

They hurried toward the front door, just as Nana walked into the entryway.

"*Kedvenc,* where are you —"

Noah didn't wait to hear the rest of her question. "Hey, Nana, we've got to run."

"Run where?"

"I'll call you later and tell you all about it," he promised as he pulled Callie out the door and into the spring air.

"Say the words," he said as they headed toward his car.

She didn't have to ask what words he meant. "I love you."

"I love you too, Callie Smith. I plan to keep reminding you of that for the rest of our lives."

EPILOGUE

Another One Bites the Dust.

Salo Wedding Curse strikes again. This time not in an aborted wedding but in an elopement. The couple believes that avoiding traditional nuptials will result in a true, happily-ever-after marriage. . . .

"Nana, it's okay." Dori kept saying the words, not that her grandmother was listening. Her grandmother had been in a state of shock ever since Noah and Callie surprised everyone by eloping. No one had even known they were dating.

When Dori said something to that effect to Callie, she'd snorted and said, *"Join the club,"* but wouldn't tell Dori what she meant by that.

"I promise, Nana —"

"Yes, promise me," her grandmother said, taking Dori's hand. "Promise me, *kedvenc,* that when the time comes, you won't care about the wedding ceremony or reception, just about the marriage. That you'll let me, or your mother, or your sister, even, plan it."

"Nana, I can guarantee that I won't care about the dress, or the cake, or any of it." Dori knew that making the promise didn't matter, because the last thing she wanted was to get married. She'd make whatever promise it took to lighten her grandmother's mood, knowing she'd never be forced to follow through with it.

Dori knew without a shadow of a doubt, she was going to be the family spinster.

"Then maybe you will break my curse, Dori."

"Nana, when my time comes" — *not that it ever would* — "you can do whatever it is you need to do to break the curse, because I won't care."

It wasn't a rash promise.

Dori Salo had long since decided, she was never going to marry.

ABOUT THE AUTHOR

Award-winning author **Holly Jacobs** has written over twenty books. She's a lifelong resident of Erie, Pennsylvania, and is happily married and has four children. She credits her family for everything she knows about love and laughter. You can visit Holly at:

www.HollyJacobs.com

or mail her at
PO Box 11102,
Erie, PA 16514-1102.

The employees of Thorndike Press hope you have enjoyed this Large Print book. All our Thorndike, Wheeler, and Kennebec Large Print titles are designed for easy reading, and all our books are made to last. Other Thorndike Press Large Print books are available at your library, through selected bookstores, or directly from us.

For information about titles, please call:
(800) 223-1244

or visit our Web site at:
http://gale.cengage.com/thorndike

To share your comments, please write:
Publisher
Thorndike Press
295 Kennedy Memorial Drive
Waterville, ME 04901